I0534484

OTHER BOOKS BY JESS MOWRY

Rats In The Trees
Children Of The Night
Way Past Cool
Six Out Seven
Ghost Train
Babylon Boyz
Phat Acceptance
Voodoo Dawgz
Bones Become Flowers
Tyger Tales
When All Goes Bright
Knights Crossing
The Bridge
Reaps
Magic Rats
Drawing From Life
Midnight Sons
Double Acting
The Coyote Valley Railroad
In The Dead Of Night
Ghost Ship
Spencer's Spirit
The Insiders
The Light

TO MRS. SINNOT

SKELETON KEY

JESS MOWRY

Copyright © 2011 - 2020 by Jess Mowry

PRINT ISBN-10: 0-9985579-3-5
PRINT ISBN-13: 978-0-9985579-3-9

EBOOK ISBN-10: 0-9977994-2-0
EBOOK ISBN-13: 978-0-9977994-2-2

First Anubis Edition 2016

SKELETON KEY

"Sleepin'! Don't give me no shit about sleepin'! Only place that boy gonna be sleepin' is six feet under the ground!"

Jarrett's eyes flew open. Had he been sleeping? It was hard to tell anymore. Half asleep or half awake, he only felt half alive.

"He's lyin'!" yelled the man outside Jarrett's door.

Yeah, thought Jarrett, struggling into consciousness like a drowned body rising through dark murky water. *I am lyin'! Lyin' here tryin' to sleep! But you never let me!*

He rubbed his eyes with the backs of his hands. They burned with the desperate need for sleep. He was always tired, nodding in class, his teachers thought he was doing drugs. As if he had any money for drugs! Even drugs that could let him sleep.

The man's voice roared in the living room: "What you tellin' me, 'thirteen dollars?' Boy holdin' on me, what he doin'! He probably buried my money somewhere!"

Jarrett squeezed his eyes tight shut, though they felt as if they were packed full of sand. *Wish I could bury YOU!* he thought. *...Wish I may, wish I might, have this wish I wish tonight.* He came close to praying. *I wish he was dead! I wish he was dead in a dirty old grave!*

Then came his mother's voice: "Leave him alone. Please. Why can't you leave him alone for one night? He got school in the mornin'. My boy need to rest."

Her tone sounded gentle, even loving. Once upon a time, Jarrett had believed that her love could protect him. Just like the moms in those fairytale stories she used to read by his bed at night. But now

1

he knew that her words, like those stories, were nothing but lies and make-believe. Only the needle she stuck in her arm was on the real anymore.

"School!" yelled the man. "Don't give me no shit about school! Boy got no time for no dumb-ass school! Boy gotta work for a livin'!"

Work! Jarrett thought, scowling in darkness. He would have worked like a slave for his mom, but he had to sell crack for the man. He wished he could lie down in peace, pull the blanket over his face and go to sleep forever. His body was so tired it hurt. He remembered something he'd heard on TV -- maybe Elmo had said it -- that it "shouldn't hurt to be a kid." But that was shit from Sesame Street, made for kids in a make-believe world, over the rainbow, behind the glass in the fantasy land of a picture tube.

His mother's voice again: "That's what he gave me. Every last penny, I swear it to God."

The man blew out a snort of disgust. "Thirteen dollars, my ass! If that really all he made today, he gonna be real unlucky tonight!"

Jarrett stared up at the shadowy ceiling. Thirteen dollars. One dollar for every year of his life. Almost worthless, like his life. Like the pennies they put on dead people's eyes. He winced despite his weariness when a wine bottle smashed on the door to his room. Were you ever too tired to be afraid?

He pushed off the blanket and slowly sat up. His movements were stiff like a zombie's as he lowered his feet to the floor. Except for his old coat lying nearby, he was dressed for the only world he knew in ragged jeans, battered sneaks, and a grimy white T-shirt tightly out-grown. He hadn't been out of those clothes for a week, and his toes felt slimy in sweat-stiffened socks. The teacher's nose had wrinkled today when she'd shaken him awake in class. He probably smelled as dead as he felt.

Again came his mother's voice: "Can't you just let him rest?"

"No rest for the wicked on this earth, bitch! Ain't you never read the Bible?"

Jarrett crept to the door. A street lamp's glimmer seeped in through the window, bathing his room with a sick yellow glow. He saw himself in the chest of drawers mirror; a boy as black as a moonless midnight with shaggy dreadlocks that smothered his shoulders and ferally framed an angular face with full pouty lips and a wide snubby nose. The tight old shirt looked painted over the high-jutting bricks of his chest, its sleeves riding high above baseball-sized biceps while baring part of a hard rippled belly. Was this how a wicked boy looked, he wondered?

Almost hidden under his hair were big haunted eyes that looked guilty of something; and he moved like a panther he'd seen in a movie, wounded by a cowardly hunter who'd been too afraid to track down his prey and finish the job of killing it.

The man's voice cursed him into a grave, but the threats had lost most of their meaning because Jarrett had heard them so often. Besides, you could only die once, and he almost didn't care if he did.

The ancient West Oakland Victorian house had tall heavy doors with old-fashioned locks. The key was in Jarrett's door now; a big brass thing called a skeleton key. Despite its spooky-sounding name it had once been a favorite toy of Jarrett's; a magical key to deep secret places with buried chests of treasure and jewels like in the stories his mom used to read. The key had seemed huge in those long-ago days, clasped gleaming like gold in his little black fingers. But he'd only been a baby then, clueless enough to believe any lies, and small enough to lie peacefully down in the long bottom drawer of his battered old dresser like a solemn young Egyptian prince at rest in a golden sarcophagus.

"He gonna be gettin' his 'rest!'" yelled the man. "Down in a grave when I done with him!"

Jarrett took hold of the key in the lock. Its smooth old shape felt familiar and warm. "Please," he whispered, and turned it softly. His mom used to scold him for locking the door. How could she save him if there was a fire? Maybe she could have saved him then, but now she couldn't even save herself.

He eased the key out of the lock and slipped it into his pocket, where it nestled beside his box-cutter knife. The man howled in rage when Jarrett did this, but all he could do was pound and kick until he got tired or finally passed out, while Jarrett shivered awake and in fear with the blanket pulled over his face.

3

Jarrett picked up a model airplane, a Douglas C-47, from the top of the chest of drawers. It had once been part of his little-kid dreams. But then he put it back down. He didn't need dreams, he just needed sleep! He gazed at the drawer that had once been his refuge, a safe place to hide from make-believe fears, like werewolves, vampires and skeletons. He wished he could slip inside again and sleep where nothing bad could get him. The wounded panther had finally found peace: it had crept down into a dark secret place, and there it had peacefully died.

The doorknob twisted viciously. The man's fist pounded the panel. "Open this door, you lyin'-ass punk! Where the rest of my money!"

The pounding continued. The kicking began. The old door shuddered and creaked in its frame. But Jarrett only walked to the window, turning his back on the cursing and rage, pressing his palms and nose to the glass like a little kid peeping a toy shop. The outside was dusted with specks of glitter, more than mist but less than rain. They gleamed like gold in the street lamp's glow, and water drops clung to a spider web, making a necklace of amber sparks. Two stories down and beyond the front yard the sidewalk glistened like polished gun-metal. Dim lights shone in a few other houses here and there along the block, but only made the night seem darker and Jarrett feel more alone. What good were other people around when no one would help you and nobody cared?

He watched as a car rolled slowly past, a long ancient car like a black station wagon and almost as big as a truck. A chill ran suddenly down his spine when he saw it was a hearse! The house next door was a funeral home, a rotting Victorian twin to his own. It looked like most of the other old houses decomposing on Jarrett's street, except for a small faded sign on its porch that advertised

Angel's Rest

But, the place had been closed before Jarrett was born, its windows boarded, its yard a jungle, its paint peeling off like a

4

mummy's skin. There were rumors of skeletons lying on basement slabs, but no kid had ever been brave enough to bust the place and check it out.

The hearse swung into the funeral home's driveway, nosing through weeds and decades of trash as if Death had returned from a long vacation.

Jarrett's door creaked as the man slammed against it. Mrs. Davis across the hall had a son who was nineteen and six feet of muscle. He had often come to Jarrett's rescue like a knight in ebony armor. But he was in the Army now and fighting terror in other lands. Mrs. Davis didn't fear the man, and had ordered the landlord to call the cops whenever he tried to beat Jarrett. But the cops wouldn't come any-more. They had finally said not to call them again, "unless the kid really got hurt."

Jarrett studied the ancient hearse though the hazy curtain of drizzle and mist. A tall slender figure, dressed all in black, emerged and seemed to scope out the 'hood. It was too dark to see many details, but the shape was clad in a long leather coat and was almost too slim for its height. Jarrett couldn't see a face, which must have been the color of night beneath an Afroish halo of hair. The shadowy movements were masculine, though graceful somehow and suggesting youth. Casually parting the waist-high weeds, the ebony figure walked to the house, climbed the steps to its high, sagging porch and vanished into darkness.

Jarrett remembered the funeral last year for his one real homey, his only true friend, a boy who'd been shot in the street for no reason. "Random violence," the cops had said, but they probably thought he'd deserved to die. The kid had looked so cool in his coffin, so peaceful and cared-for and clean... which wasn't at all how he'd looked when alive. He'd seemed safely asleep in his very own box, soft satin-lined and just the right size to rest in peace for eternity.

Jarrett shivered, still scanning the hearse while clutching the key in his pocket. His room smelled of dampness and ancient decay. A grave would probably smell like that. But, at least underground in a coffin, nobody was trying to kill you.

5

The man slammed a shoulder against the door. "Where my money, little bitch!"

Jarrett spread helpless hands and turned to face the door. Trying to reason just made it worse, but he couldn't stay silent. "I give it to mom, like always."

"You made more'n thirteen dollars today!"

Too tired to think, Jarrett clenched his fists. His voice rose high before he could stop it. "That shit you make me sell! Who gonna buy it 'cept dumb little kids! What kind of money you figure they got?"

"You DEAD, boy!" snarled the man.

Jarrett's hand went to his pocket again, gripping the key in cold sweaty fingers. "Please," he whispered. "Somebody help me!"

But no one could hear him. Or cared if they did. He might as well have *been* in a grave and crying for help under six feet of dirt. The air in the room seemed to ripple with rage. The door panel cracked with a gunfire sound as the man crashed against it again. Jarrett stared in sudden horror as a jagged gash like a lightning-bolt appeared in the age-blackened wood.

"Dead boy!"

Jarrett spun back to the window. Grabbing the handles, he struggled to raise it, but a week of wet weather had swollen it shut! Sweat broke out on his body while tears trickled hot down his cheeks. He battled the window with all his strength, but it wouldn't open! He shot another a look over his shoulder... light leaked in through the splintered door. He heard the man stagger to ram it again. Jarrett swung a desperate fist and smashed the gold-speckled glass, but shards ripped his arm when he jerked it back. For a second he stared at his own dripping blood while steam wavered pale in the cold. Then he lifted his eyes to the hole in the glass and the razor-edged daggers still stuck in the frame. Should he throw himself through like they did in movies? But, what if he cut his throat?

At his back came a crash as the door burst open! Dim yellow light fanned into the room, and a shadow stretched over the dusty floor, lurching in Jarrett's direction. What did it matter now? he thought. Throwing an arm in front of his face, he poised to leap through the window.

6

A hand grabbed his shoulder. "Dead boy!"

TWO

Jarett struggled savagely like something wild in a trap. The man rammed a knee between Jarrett's legs and the sickening pain seemed to suck out his strength. The man's grip loosened a little as if he thought he'd won, but Jarrett had expected that. He tore himself free and tried to run, but the man caught a handful of his shirt. Jarrett fought like a panther, kicking, scratching, trying to bite. The old cotton ripped and he dashed out the doorway, his shoulder clawed by the man's fingernails.

His mother sat on the living room couch seemingly lost in the TV world, and he didn't waste time by running to her; she couldn't help him anymore. He caught a glimpse of kids at McDonalds begging their parents for Happy Meals as he darted to the hallway door and fought with the three heavy bolts. One slid back, but he heard the man coming! Then he got the second bolt open. He saw his mother turn to him.

"Don't forget your jacket, honey."

The last bolt slid back. Jarrett flung the door open, but a hand shot out and slammed it again! Jarrett leaped sideways and dug in his pocket, grabbing his box-cutter knife. The man swung a fist but Jarrett ducked, then whipped out his blade and slashed the man's arm. The man roared in pain but drunkenly dodged as Jarrett tried to cut him again, his own wounded arm spraying bright ruby drops. Jarrett retreated, yanked the door open and dashed down the hall to the staircase. The man burst out to clumsily follow, stumbling, staggering, slamming the walls. Jarrett slipped at the top of the stairs and grabbed the rickety banister post. The man's fist caught him

8

square in the back, knocking him down in a cart-wheeling tumble of wildly flying arms and legs to slam the wall of the landing below.

His head hit hard, scattering chunks of plaster that clattered around him like brittle old bones. Sparks exploded somewhere in his skull. The box-knife slipped from his bloody fingers. For a moment he was lost in darkness, but he fought his eyes into focus again, gritted his teeth and rolled onto his back. His wounded arm was pouring blood, smearing the floor as he sprawled in the corner.

In the hallway above the man swayed on his feet, almost falling himself. He lurched against the banister and grabbed the post, tearing it loose. Jarrett lay gasping for breath, trying to make his body work, to force it to get up and run.

The man slowly hefted the wooden post. "You a dead boy!"

A light bulb silhouetted the man as he stalked unsteadily down the stairs. Jarrett struggled to rise, but something was wrong... it hurt like fire to move his left foot! Sobbing, he managed to get to his knees. He searched for his knife in the shadows... *there!* He grabbed it and tried to crawl down the steps, but a hand clutched his sneaker, dragging him back. He heard the hiss of the club cutting air and frantically flung himself aside. The club missed his head but grazed his arm, stabbing a new shock of pain. He lashed out hard with his other foot. The man yelled a curse and let go.

Jarrett tried to dive down the stairs, but the man grabbed the ragged remains of his shirt and whipped back the club to hit him again. Jarrett curled up, protecting his head, but the club hit the wall and plaster rained down. Jarrett crawled into the corner, huddling there as the club swung again but missed by an inch and hit the wall. He slashed out blind with his knife, feeling flesh rip across the man's thigh. The man dropped the club and clutched his leg, stumbling against the banister. Ancient wood splintered. The man let out a terrified scream and toppled into the stairwell.

The crash seemed to take forever in coming. Jarrett collapsed in the corner, gasping, crying, fighting for breath. His shirt was in shreds like zombie rags, and the boards beneath him were slick with his blood. His ribs felt like the banister looked, matching the pain between his legs, while his ankle burned with bolts of fire. He heard the club roll down the stairs, thudding slowly one at a time like a severed head in an old horror movie. A minute passed while he struggled to breathe. Finally, he got to his hands and knees and crawled to the edge of the landing. Dimly seen in the shadows below, the man lay sprawled on his back.

"Please," Jarrett whispered, not sure what he meant. The man moved a little and moaned. His fingers clutched empty space like a baby's. Then, Jarrett heard Mrs. Davis above furiously pounding the landlord's door:

"Call 'em!" she yelled. "I don't care what they said! Tell 'em he's killin' the boy this time!"

There were other voices in rooms below, confused, angry, waken-ed from sleep, afraid to open their own locked doors to help a wicked and worthless kid.

Forgetting his knife, Jarrett gripped the remains of the banister and pulled himself to his feet. He almost screamed from the pain in his ankle, but clenched his teeth and made it support him. He started down, dragging a shoulder along the wall and leaving a bloody smear. More blood from his arm dripped a glistening trail.

The man's eyes were open, but smoky and glazed in the glow of a feeble light bulb. They didn't seem to see Jarrett as he reached the foot of the stairs. Jarrett stood for a moment panting for breath. He scanned the man's face in the dimness, but the empty eyes, like a corpse's, seemed to look off in some distant direction.

He became aware of voices again, fading in and out on the edge of hearing like a far-away radio station at night. Strange-looking shadows moved on the walls. Jarrett knew he had to get out. The man was dying -- Jarrett knew that without knowing how -- and he was the killer! The cops wouldn't care about anything else; he was just another black boy to catch and lock up in a cage! He stumbled away, dragging his foot, struggling toward the house's front door. Then he was out in the drizzly night. The cold and dampness burned his wounds. The door clicked shut and locked behind him, but that was better than being locked in.

He almost fell, but caught the porch rail. He clung there a minute, panting. His jeans had slipped low on his blood-slicked hips, and his half-naked body was chilled by the air. His rasping breath made smoky puffs that floated in front of his face, while steam curled up from his bleeding arm. He wondered if the thickening mist was incoming fog, or just in his mind. The street lamps glimmered eerily pale. A siren sounded somewhere in the distance, echoing hollowly in his ears.

Jarrett scanned the deserted street as best he could with his fading sight. The mist was rising up the stairs like a silent gray sea. Then it crept icily over him, blurring his eyes, thick in his lungs, making it even harder to breathe. But the siren was coming! His bloody hand went to his pocket, gripping the friendly old shape of the key. It felt warm to his touch... the only warm thing in the world. New tears filled his eyes as he limped down the steps to the trash-littered sidewalk.

The houses around him were tottering shapes that seemed to lean over and threaten. The street lamps were nothing but yellowish blurs. Jarrett fled from the oncoming siren, a hand groping out like a blind boy lost. He slammed into something; a big looming shadow of night-colored steel beaded with droplets of drizzle and fog. He saw it was the ancient hearse and lurched away in horror. He would have run if he'd had the strength, but could only stumble through fog.

An alley gaped like a black empty mouth. The siren sound had faded, but someone was probably after him. He staggered into the alley. Rotting garbage slid underfoot. Rats scuttled squeaking unseen in the dark. He stopped at a Dumpster, clutching its coldness, pressing his chest to the wet rusty steel. He wondered if he could hide in there like trash among trash. But, something about those double lids was like a ghostly memory and terrified him as much as the hearse. The alley's far end was a pale shade of black, and he limped toward the light, faint as it was.

Out on another shadow-filled street. Why were all the lights so dim? A car went by in a mumbling blur. Its headlights seemed no brighter than candles but left the night darker when they had passed. He wondered why he wasn't cold -- his dreadlocks wetly framed his face, and his shirt was no more than sodden shreds -- and yet he only felt tired. All he wanted to do was sleep, but he stumbled on from nothing to nowhere for what seemed like an eternity.

Something smashed into his face! Staggering back, he crashed to the ground. The man's words echoed again in his ears: *dead boy!*

Too tired to care, he closed his eyes and quietly lay on the cold concrete like a corpse on a slab in a morgue.

THREE

Time crept by like coffin worms crawling on a corpse. It might have been hours or could have been years, but nothing hit Jarrett again. Maybe he actually slept for a while. But at last, and almost reluctantly, he finally opened his eyes. His vision came slowly into focus like the opening scene of a movie. For a minute he lay there on his back in the dim yellow glow of an old street lamp on a telephone pole. He heard the sputtering buzz of wet wires and the soft liquid sound of trickling water. He became aware of pain again -- his ankle, his arm, between his legs -- as he raised his head to look around.

He was sprawled on a cracked and buckled sidewalk where weeds grew tall between the slabs, and the cold was seeping into his bones. He realized no one had hit him; he'd only walked blindly into the pole. He grasped its mossy rotting wood and dragged himself to his feet. His ankle burned with flares of fire but he tried to ignore the pain. He checked his arm, which only seemed to be oozing blood, then scanned around again. A stab of panic shot through him when he found he didn't know where he was.

The street was in no better shape than the sidewalk, its pavement a jagged mosaic of cracks. The gutters were choked with years of trash, and the weeds had grown unchallenged. It was an empty, dead-end street; and a new chill suddenly traced his spine when he saw where it dead-ended at...

The tall iron gates of a graveyard!

The place was ancient and looked forgotten in a dark deserted neighborhood of boarded-up houses and old factories. Beyond the

13

cone of the street lamp's glow were the massive, rusted, wrought-iron gates. They were set in a seven-foot wall of brick, covered with ivy and slowly collapsing but still defending the dead. Jarrett limped up to the gates and grasped the cold bars to look in.

The graveyard was small and a jungle of weeds, a lawn gone wild, and blackberry vines. Tilted tombstones reared through the grass like rotted fangs in an animal skull. Scattered among them were tottering statues. Jarrett supposed they were angels, but none looked friendly in the dark. A pond glimmered back in the shadows, with another small statue set in its center. The trickle of water came faintly, and except for the crackle of wires overhead it seemed to be the only sound. Among the crumbling monuments stood little stone houses of various shapes. They didn't seem to have any windows... but no one inside would need look out. Yet, they seemed to offer safety and peace, protected by walls and defended by gates. One little house way in the back even had a tiny front porch.

Jarrett gazed through the iron bars and suddenly wished he could go to that house, to sleep among people who couldn't hurt him. He studied the gates as he thought about that, but he was too weak to climb over, and they were held shut by a massive old chain secured with a huge padlock.

He finally sank down with his back to the bars. Wherever he was, he'd come too far and there was nowhere else to go. He drew the skeleton key from his pocket, not knowing why except it felt warm, the only warm thing in the world. "Please," he whispered to no one.

"Yo!" called a voice in the darkness.

Jarrett tensed with a new stab of fear. But his moment of panic passed when he realized the voice was a kid's. He turned around and peered through the gates. A chubby boy sat on a mossy tombstone maybe twenty feet away.

Trying to fight the pain in his ankle, Jarrett pulled himself to his feet. The street lamp's glow didn't reach very far, and the boy sat in shadow cast by the wall, but he didn't look any older than Jarrett.

Jarrett stood there gripping the bars, not even sure if the boy was real or something called up by his own battered mind. "Um... S'up, man?" he finally asked.

The boy smiled and opened a palm toward the sky. "Moon, stars, an' us."

Jarrett stared at the chubby kid sitting so casually cool on the tombstone, then looked up to see only darkness. "It's kinda rainy tonight."

"Moon an' stars always up there, bro, even if you can't always see 'em."

Jarrett tried to smile back. He wished he wasn't hurting so much so his smile could be more on the real. His voice sounded hollow and strange in his ears, as if he was talking from far away and only hearing an echo. "Well... um... guess there's some things you don't gotta see. But they there anyhow, like you said."

"Maybe like God?" asked the boy.

Jarrett shrugged. "God never believed in me, so why should I believe in Him? ...Do you?"

"Sometimes," said the boy. "But I ain't very religious."

Jarrett forced another smile. He knew he looked like a bloody corpse, and didn't want to scare the kid. "Um... I be in somebody's ground, man? Guess I'm kinda lost."

Far from being freaked by Jarrett, the chubby boy only smiled again, as if talking to bloody, beat-up kids was something he did every night. He indicated the silent graveyard with the wave of a hand. "Ain't nobody in this ol' ground gonna cap your ass for trespassin'."

Jarrett felt the boy's friendliness like a warm breath of breeze in the night. "Guess not, huh. ...So, how you know I was out here?"

"Seen you from my window."

Jarrett peered into the mist... was there a caretaker's house?

The boy hopped down from the tombstone and sauntered casually up to the gates into the feeble street light glow. He had skin of a honey-bronze shade and that rolly-poly look of soft fat draped on a small skeleton, with boy-breasts bobbing like melons of Jell-O underneath an old black T-shirt almost cartoonishly too tight, while his belly hung out more than half bare twin scalloped shapes like a plump baby's bottom displaying the funnel-like cave of a navel. He wore ragged jeans with one ripped knee, tightly outgrown, mostly unbuttoned, and baring the brassy moons of his butt. His feet were encased in huge ancient sneaks that seemed to be falling apart and were wrapped with electrical tape on the toes. His hair was a natural bush of curls that shadowed a cheerfully chubby-cheeked face with a wide button nose and full pouty lips.

Jarrett thought of a fat lion cub, though he tagged the kid as a solo street-rat who didn't belong to anyone's posse. Still, it was safer to ask: "Are you in a gang?"

The chubby boy leaned against the gates and rested an arm on the rusty chain. He had gold-tinted eyes that now seemed to sadden. "Used to be, but not no more. Shit happens, y'know."

Jarrett nodded. Hurt as he was, it still felt good to have someone to talk to. "Got that right."

The boy studied Jarrett. "Looks like *you* got in some serious shit. ...It cool if you need to cry, man. I still do sometimes."

"Nah," sighed Jarrett. "Seem like a waste of somethin'. ...Um, so there's a house in there?"

The boy aimed a thumb over his shoulder. "That little stone house with the porch."

Despite his thoughts of safety and peace, a skeleton finger traced Jarrett's spine. "You live in *there?*"

"Ain't much of a goin'-on neighborhood, huh?"

"Mean you homeless?" asked Jarrett.

The boy thumbed the shadowed valley between the opulent orbs of his chest. "Just me, myself an' I."

"Well..." said Jarrett. "'Least nobody beatin' on you in there." He shivered again, and his teeth almost rattled. Then he felt a flicker of hope. "Can I come in an' stay with you? I don't got nowhere else to go."

The boy checked Jarrett once more. "This might not be the coolest place for somebody in the shape you in. Hate to say it, doggie-bro, but I can almost see right through ya."

Jarrett didn't know what that meant, but he didn't like the sound of it. He looked down at himself, seeing the ribbon-like rags of his shirt. "I probably look like a zombie, huh?"

"I seen scarier things," said the boy. "But if I was you I'd find me

16

some help."

"Ain't no help for me," said Jarrett. "Let me come in with you. Please."

"How you gonna get in?" asked the boy.

"How'd you get in?" asked Jarrett.

"I don't think you up for that tonight."

Jarrett regarded the gates again, knowing he couldn't climb over with his wounded arm and twisted ankle. "Can you help me?"

The boy spread his hands. "How?"

"Well... could you come out an' give me a boost?"

"I don't think I can do that."

"Why not?" asked Jarrett.

"I ain't very physical, see?" The boy struck a body-builder pose, comically puffing his boy-breasts and flexing his chub-padded arms. His shirt climbed high above his belly and now looked a bit like a bra.

Jarrett would have laughed if he could, but it seemed to get harder to make his voice work, and it sounded even more like an echo. "Please, man!"

"Why don't you try that?" asked the boy.

"Huh?" Jarrett looked down at the big brass key still gripped in his bloody fingers. "This? It only open the door to my room."

"It's a skeleton key," said the boy, tapping it with a fingertip. "They can open lots of things."

Jarrett studied the huge padlock, brass like his key but green with age. The keyhole did seem about the right size. He slipped the key in, surprised when it fit, but paused before trying to turn it. "Um... so it's cool, man? ...Me comin' in if my key works?"

"Can't think of nothin' else you can do." The boy scanned Jarrett again. "Hate to say it, doggie-bro, but you probably gonna die tonight if you stay out there all wet an' cold."

Jarrett shrugged, making no move to turn the key. "Maybe that's better, my life wasn't shit."

The boy looked sad. "I used to think dyin' was a way out, too."

A tear slid coldly down Jarrett's cheek. He suddenly blurted, "I killed somebody tonight, man! It was a accident, swear to God! But

17

the cops gonna call it murder!"

The boy didn't seem surprised. "Figured it was somethin' like that; you got a haunted look."

Jarrett let go of the key, leaving it in the lock. He turned away and shrugged again. "Maybe I should just sit down an' die." He looked over his shoulder. "You gonna watch?"

The boy also shrugged. "Guess there's nothin' else I can do, if that's what you really want. I seen some other kids die, an' I couldn't do nothin' about that either."

"So, what if my key don't work?"

"Then you done all you can," said the boy. "But it's stupid if you don't try it, man, 'cause you don't look no older than me."

"What difference that make?" asked Jarrett. "Kids die every day."

The boy spread his hands. "How can you think about dyin' when you don't really know about livin'?"

Jarrett spit on the sidewalk. "I know livin' hurts, an' I'm tired of hurtin'! I call that knowin' enough! ...Guess I'm just wicked, is all. Maybe dyin's the only way I can rest."

"You don't look wicked to me," said the boy, "an' I know wicked when I see it."

Jarrett scowled. "Aw, leave me the hell alone, man! Let me die in peace at least."

"If that's what you want." The boy returned to the tombstone and perched his rolly shape on top like a little Buddha. He pulled out a crumpled pack of Kools and fired one with a wooden match. The flame lit his face like a study in bronze. He puffed a ghost of smoke at the sky, then spread his arms to take in the graveyard. "A lot of these people never checked out what their keys could open before they did."

Jarrett wiped his eyes. "Now what you babblin' about?"

The boy aimed his cigarette ember at Jarrett. "Did you have a choice of where you was born?"

"'Course I didn't!"

"An' who your folks was? An' where you come up?"

Jarrett snorted. "An' what color I wanted to be?"

"Well, give that boy a big fat cee-gar."

"Oh, shut up, man!"

"But you gots a key an' you ain't even tried it."

"You crazy?" Jarrett suddenly yelled. "Talkin' 'bout keys an' cigars an' shit when I'm out here dyin' an' you won't help me!"

"This is me tryin' to help," said the boy. "But I can't throw your dumb ass over them gates. Check yourself, man. Standin' out there with a key in your hand an' cryin' you ready to die."

"I ain't cryin', fool!"

The boy shook his head. "Shit, you don't deserve any rest. 'Wicked?' My ass! Y'all just a snotnose baby, man! You just like all them thugger fools! Cryin' you got it so hard in life but not doin' nothin' to change it."

"I *can't* change it!"

The boy blew a smoke ring, pale in the dark. "Where there's life, there's always hope."

"That just a old sayin'."

"Just 'cause somethin's old don't mean it can't relate to you."

Jarrett shivered. It seemed stupid to be dying and arguing about it. He grabbed the key and turned it. The lock fell suddenly open and the chain clanked loose against the bars. The boy plopped down from the tombstone and came to the gates with a smile.

"So, what you waitin' for?" The boy waved around at the statues. "Think these angels gonna sing 'cause you done somethin' you shoulda done?"

Jarrett shoved on the rusty bars, and the gates swung open with a gritty scream. The chubby boy giggled. "Careful, man, you might wake the dead."

FOUR

Jarrett stumbled into the graveyard, lurching like a wounded zombie. The chubby boy steadied him, gripping his shoulders. "Better lock the gates, man, people dyin' to get in here."

Jarrett managed the ghost of a smile and pushed the gates creakingly shut. He linked the lock through the chain again and held it closed while turning the key.

The boy offered a hand. "I'm Robby."

"Jarrett," said Jarrett, doing the old-school shake with Robby, whose hand felt as warm as the skeleton key.

"Yo, Jarrett," said Robby, "lean on me."

Jarrett's ankle was stabbing pain, but with an arm over Robby's shoulders he managed a slow limping walk. Robby smelled like a homeless kid -- like he probably smelled, Jarrett thought -- dirty jeans, grungy sneaks, and strong boy-scent sort of damp-dirt earthy. They went up a faint path in the drifting mist through knee-high grass and waist-high weeds, past crumbling tombs and monuments to the little stone house at the back of the grounds. Robby helped Jarrett climb to the porch, which was heavily shrouded in blackberry vines. Jarrett imagined how it might look on a warm and sunny afternoon, a peace-ful place of leafy shade, but he saw no backpack or sleeping bag to show where Robby cribbed.

"Where…?" he started to ask.

"Inside."

"Huh?" Jarrett stared at the vine-covered crypt. He'd been wrong about windows, the place had one, small and set in a heavy iron door. It might have been made of colored glass like something he'd

20

seen in a church but he couldn't be sure in the dark. "You sleep in *there?*" he said with a shiver.

Robby smiled. "Better than sleepin' with the fishes."

Out on the street, lost and alone, the little stone house had looked safe to Jarrett, but now inside this place of death it looked exactly what it was. "But, that's a *grave*, man! ...Sorta."

"Give that boy another cee-gar."

"...But, it's full of dead people an' skeletons!"

Robby rolled his eyes. "They prefer the term, 'living impaired.' An', 'case you ain't noticed, there's nothin' *but* dead people here. What difference it make if you sleep outside or snuggle up close? If you don't get out them wet ol' rags an' warm your ass up real soon, you gonna be sleepin' with skeletons till all the stars go out."

Jarrett shivered again. "But, it's scary!"

Robby shrugged. "Life is scary, like I'm sure you noticed. But nothin' in there's gonna hurt you."

Jarrett grasped the iron door handle. The hinges were rusted almost solid, and it took nearly every bit of his strength to pull the door squealing open a little. Then it seemed to jam with a clank. "Yo, Robby," he panted. "There's a chain on it, man."

Robby nodded. "They used to do that in the ol' days. So the door would stay open a little but grave-robbers couldn't get in."

"Why would they wanna leave the door open?"

"So if someone got buried alive they could scream."

"Maaaaan!"

Robby gave Jarrett a nudge. "Stop wussin' out an' get inside before you take the nap that rots."

The heavy chain was stiff with rust, but Jarrett managed to loosen it by yanking on the door a few times. Then he turned sideways and wiggled through, his chest plates skinning moss from the door frame. The crypt was black as death inside and he couldn't see a thing. He sniffed the air uneasily, not sure what he expected to smell, but there was only the dry scent of dust. He whispered to Robby, almost afraid he'd wake something up by talking too loud. "Got a match?"

Robby giggled from out on the porch. "Not since Superman

died."

"Yo, c'mon, man," said Jarrett. "This no time for clownin'."

"Sorry," said Robby. "There's a candle back in the corner. Hang on an' I light it."

Jarrett took a few steps with his hands stretched out, then stood in the darkness, waiting. He couldn't see Robby slip past him, though he felt a small sensation of warmth and scented grungy boy smell for a moment. There was a soft scratching sound, then a feeble blue spark and a curse.

"Damn old matches!" said Robby.

Jarrett moved toward Robby's voice. "I got some... aw shit, they wet!"

Robby giggled again, friendly echoes that mocked the silence. Jarrett was starting to like that sound; it was somehow free and alive. "Now what's funny?" he asked.

"I forgot," said Robby.

"Forgot what?"

"Sometimes I'm a little retarded. I got other matches right here in my pocket."

A yellow flare scattered the shadows, lighting Robby's chubby face as he crouched in a cobwebby corner. He touched the flame to a candle stub that was stuck in a forty-ounce bottle. The wick resisted a second or two, then a golden glow spread though the tomb. Jarrett saw long marble slabs on the walls, each with handles like drawers on a dresser. Bracketed between them were little brass vases, a few still holding mummified flowers.

The candle flame dazzled Jarrett's eyes after so many hours in darkness, but the light brought a feeling of peace. He limped to the door and dragged it shut. He noticed a keyhole and pulled out his key, feeling relieved when it fit. The works turned with a squeak and locked like a bite.

Robby had stayed by the candle, his palms held out to the tiny flame as if it could really provide any warmth. "Feel safe now?"

Jarrett looked around. "Funny. Like, here I am in a grave, but this the first time I felt safe in a year." He met Robby's eyes, gold in the light. "Thanks for lettin' me come in."

"It was your key got you in," said Robby.

Jarrett looked down at himself, his shirt in shreds, his blood-spattered jeans, the gash on his arm still oozing red. "So, you don't think I'm gonna die?"

"Someday for sure, but not tonight maybe. "Least not if we get you warm an' dry. An' you look hella strong with all them muscles."

Jarrett shrugged. "I don't feel very strong."

"Think strong thoughts an' get out them wet rags."

"You mean get naked in here?"

Robby thumped a marble slab with his fist. "The skeletons ain't gonna get jealous 'cause you got skin on your bones."

Jarrett saw blankets in a corner. There was also a stack of dusty comics, along with some books that were massive and old. Glancing around at the ominous slabs, he stripped off the sodden remains of his shirt, then sat on the floor to untie his sneaks. He found his body was painfully stiff as he tried to reach his feet.

"Yo," said Robby. "Let me do that."

Robby removed Jarrett's shoes and socks, then helped him take off his jeans. Jarrett's ebony skin made a stark contrast to the pale white stone all around. Robby wrapped him in a blanket, then spread another on the floor.

"Lay down," said Robby. "I check out your foot."

Jarrett's ankle still hurt like fire, but Robby clasped it in both hands and the pain subsided a little. Robby's fingers moved expertly, pres-sing, massaging here and there. "Might not be too bad," he said. "Really ain't swollen a lot."

Jarrett sighed. "Feels better with you doin' that."

"My mom done that for me," said Robby. "When I twisted my ankle skateboardin'."

"My mom used to do that stuff," said Jarrett, relaxing with his back to one of the long marble slabs.

"Used to?" asked Robby.

"She... a junkie now, man. She don't do nothin' no more."

"Oh," said Robby. "Sorry, man. What about your dad?"

"He got killed in the Army. Fightin' the war on terror."

"Sorry," said Robby again. "Your life ain't been easy."

23

Jarrett shrugged. "It wasn't so bad a year ago. But then some shit-slangin' punk come around an' put the moves on my mom. ...He's the one I killed tonight. It was an accident, like I said, but the cops gonna call it murder."

"Don't worry about that now," said Robby. "Wish I had somethin' to clean your arm, but it ain't bleedin' much anymore."

"I probably don't got a lot of blood left."

Robby laughed. "Yeah, you white as a ghost."

The blanket on stone felt as soft as feathers as Jarrett lay down and relaxed. "But, where you gonna sleep, Robby? I can't take both your blankets."

"Don't worry about it, I'm used to the cold."

"Those your books an' comics?" asked Jarrett.

"Nah. They belong to a homey of mine. Name's Eric."

"He collect comics?" asked Jarrett. "That a classic ol' *Tales From The Crypt.*"

"Yeah," said Robby. "He like spooky stuff. He used to spend the nights with me. Read ghost stories or told 'em himself, an' give me the haps on the rest of the crew."

"The gang you were in?" asked Jarrett.

Robby seemed to think for a moment. "It was more like a gang that wasn't. Just friends who watched each other's backs."

"Don't Eric come see you no more?"

Robby looked at the iron door. "Not for a while. But, he's gonna come back pretty soon."

"Think so?" asked Jarrett, also glancing toward the door as if expecting a knock. "Gotta be way past midnight."

"He always come real late," said Robby. "Sometimes I wait by the gates."

"Oh," said Jarrett. "I kinda wondered what you was doin', sittin' out there in the dark."

"Seen you from my window. Didn't I say that already?"

"Yeah."

Robby shrugged. "I forget stuff. Like, things I said, an' when I said 'em."

"You smoke a lotta weed?"

24

"Nah. Forgettin' for me is a natural thing."

"Mean you done it all your life?"

Robby smiled. "I forgot if I did. But, I got dropped on my head once. Like when I was little." He tapped the top of his head with a finger. "My skull's a little flat on top, but I guess you can't see that now."

"Think somethin' happened to Eric?"

"Nah," said Robby. "He was into magic an' spirit stuff. Could feel bad things before they happened. Besides, he never went lookin' for shit."

"I didn't either," said Jarrett. "But it found me anyhow."

"Shit's always out there," said Robby. "An' bad shit still happens to good people. But if you ever meet Eric you'll see it don't happen much to him. He probably scare you at first, but he's cool."

Jarrett was getting sleepy, but he was also curious about this homeless boy. "What you mean by magic, Robby? Like, pullin' rabbits out hats?"

"He never done that," said Robby. "I mean, he *could* if he wanted to. But he was more into African magic. Like in that voodoo book over there." Robby giggled again. "An' what you gonna do with a rabbit once it come out the hat?"

"Don't it go back in?" asked Jarrett.

"Ever see one go back in?"

Jarrett considered. "Guess not, huh? Like, the magician just pulls 'em out an' gives 'em to his helper or somethin'."

Robby nodded. "There's lots of things that never go back after you pull 'em out."

Jarrett closed his eyes for a moment. The blanket on stone felt so soft. "I know it ain't cool to axe, but what happen to your parents?"

Robby sat down with his back to a slab, one of twelve that lined the tomb, four on each wall except for the front. "The usual shit. The kind that happen all the time till it finally happen to you. My dad couldn't find any work, an' he finally give up lookin' an' left. My mom had to work two jobs."

"So did mine," sighed Jarrett. "Before... you know... the shit."

"I ain't forgot," said Robby. "But my mom got tired of livin', I

25

guess."

"What you mean?"

"She died."

"...Oh. Sorry, man."

Robby went on, 'The cops locked me up for awhile. That was so they could help me adjust, but it just got me more unadjusted. Then they put me in a home. But nothin's a home when they lock you in."

"What happened?" asked Jarrett.

"They didn't lock me in good enough."

"You like livin' in a graveyard better than a home?"

"Gives me lots of time to read."

"I used to read a lot," said Jarrett. "But then I didn't have time no more."

"Speakin' of time," said Robby. "You better get some sleep, doggie-bro. There's lots of time tomorrow."

Jarrett wanted to listen to Robby, the first friendly voice he'd heard in months. But he seemed to be floating away on clouds and his eyes were slowly closing.

FIVE

Jarrett woke up to a rainbow. Blinking his eyes in wonder, he raised himself on his elbows and looked around in the pretty light. For a moment he felt a flash of fear, finding himself surrounded by stone in a space the size of a prison cell, but then he remembered where he was.

Sunlight shone in through the colored-glass window, and dust motes danced in the multi-hued beams. It seemed funny to think he'd slept in a grave and actually rested in peace. He sat up slowly and rubbed his eyes, almost surprised they didn't feel scratchy. His naked body was stiff and sore, his ankle and ribs still hurt when he moved, but he'd been hurt many times in his life and knew the pain would pass. He checked his arm, a mess of dried blood. But there probably weren't any germs in here with nothing alive to live on. He noticed his bloody jeans and the ragged remains of his shirt had been hung on one of the little brass vases. Then he suddenly stared around.

"Robby?" His voice echoed back from silent stone. He turned to the corner behind him... just the old comics, the big dusty books, and the candle stub in the forty-ounce bottle. Shoving off the blanket, he scrambled stiffly to his feet. His ankle throbbed as if stuck with needles, but seemed strong enough to support him. "Robby?" he called again.

He felt a little dizzy. He swayed, and put a hand on the wall. His fingers found a cold brass handle -- like a pull on his chest of drawers at home -- and he jerked his hand away. That was probably stupid; those slabs were sealed with cement, and there wasn't much chance

27

he could open one for an unwanted peep at a skeleton!

He noticed the dusty letters and numbers carved in the blue-veined marble; the meaningless names and birth and death dates of people long-dead and maybe forgotten. It was strange to think that the bones in here had all been kids a long time ago.

After a minute the dizziness passed and he saw his key was still in the lock. He limped the few steps to the door. The thick iron plates were warm from the sun. He unlocked the lock, then, straining against the rusty hinges, he pushed the heavy door open. He felt another moment of fear when the door seemed to jam and wouldn't budge, but then he remembered the chain. Twisting his body sideways, his chest plates skimming moss from the frame, he wiggled through into the light.

Just as he'd imagined last night, the crypt's front porch was peacefully lit by a soft green glow through the blackberry vines. He stood for a time on a carpet of leaves to savor the fresh morning air. It was almost a new experience, or maybe one he'd forgotten. Then he returned to the tomb. The shreds of his shirt were beyond any use, but his blood-stained jeans were fairly dry. He pulled them on, then, carrying his sneaks and socks, he went to the door and squeezed out again. He slipped the key into his pocket and descended the single stone step. He paused once more to stand in the sunlight, enjoying its warmth on his ebony skin like something else he hardly remembered. Water drops gleamed in the shade of gravestones, and the air smelled of spring and young growing things. Bees hovered over pretty wild-flowers and lavender-tinted blackberry blossoms while making a drowsy droning sound. The liquid music of trickling water came from the lily-filled pond. The big dirty city was lurking out there beyond the crumbling, mossy-bricked walls, but its outlines seemed hazy and almost unreal. He could hear city sounds if he listened -- the rumble of traffic, a siren's scream -- but around him were only the buzzing of bees, the music of water, the chirping of birds. He brushed back his blood-matted dreadlocks, then, shading his eyes with a hand, he scanned around the tombstones.

"Robby!" he called.

"Yo." Robby stepped from the shadows of blackberry vines that thickly shrouded the crypt. Seen in sunlight, his skin seemed to glow, and his eyes held a bright gleam of gold. His belly jiggled with every step like the cliché about Jell-O, spilling way over his half-buttoned jeans like the cheerfully lolling tongue of a puppy, and a boy-breast bobbed out of a big ragged hole in the front of his faded black T-shirt. He grinned as he came up to Jarrett. "Guess you decided not to die."

Jarrett smiled. "Didn't think I had a choice. But you were there to keep me alive."

Robby looked thoughtful. "Hate to say it, doggie-bro, but I wasn't sure you was gonna make it. I watched you after you fell asleep."

Jarrett smiled again: in some other place it might have seemed strange for another dude to watch over him, but here it felt totally natural. He stretched in the golden sunlight, wincing a bit from the pain in his ribs, but nothing seemed to be broken. "I probably *would* of been worm-food if you hadn't let me come in."

"Cool you decided to use your key." Robby plopped down on the slab of a tomb, his belly spilling into his lap, his bottom plumply part bare on the stone. "So, what you gonna do now?"

Jarrett's smile died on his lips: he'd felt so good waking up alive that he'd almost forgotten the shit he was in. "I... don't know." Something rumbled softly, like the sleepy growl of a jungle cat, and he patted his stony stomach. "I think I'm kinda hungry."

Robby giggled. "Ain't nothin' much to dig up in here, 'less you want a rack of ribs."

Jarrett made a face. "Another graveyard joke?"

"The dead are easily amused."

Jarrett sat down next to Robby. The weathered old granite was comfortably warm, and the sun felt good on his skin. He gently poked Robby's belly, his finger sinking half out of sight. "Looks like you livin' large, man. How you been gettin' by?"

"I always been fat," said Robby. "Wouldn't be me if I wasn't."

"But, how you manage to stay fat? Homeless kids are skin an' bones."

Robby seemed to think for a moment. "After I run away, I hooked up with some other dudes."

29

"The gang that wasn't?" asked Jarrett.

"Yeah, I remember. I was eatin' big-time at Donny's." Robby seemed to think again. "Yeah, Donny. …His mom worked at a Safeway an' brung home tons of damaged stuff, like Twinkies, Ding-Dongs an' Ho-Hos."

"You look cool bein' fat," said Jarrett.

Robby spread his arms. "Mom used to say there was more to love. But, too bad you never met Donny. He was the fattest kid in the world! But I always thought he looked cool that way. Like, maybe God wanted him to be fat so he could be…"

"What?" asked Jarrett.

"Himself," said Robby, after a moment. "He read tons of books an' knew a lot about a lot. An' fat kids don't usually get in trouble."

Jarrett looked down at his hard-muscled body. "Maybe you right about that. Did Donny come here an' see you like Eric?"

"He wanted to, but he was too fat to climb over the gates."

Jarrett pulled up a flower and started to pick off the petals. "I like this place, Robby. You was smart comin' here. But, why you decide to live in a graveyard? Sure it's peaceful an' safe, an' I guess you ain't scared of ghosts, but don't you get lonely sometimes?"

Robby looked up at the sun. "Remember what I said last night? About seein' kids die? …I did say that, didn't I?"

"Yeah."

Robby gazed at the sun and his golden eyes saddened. "I killed a kid, man. …I didn't want to, but I don't think I had any choice."

"…Oh."

Robby faced the hazy city out beyond the walls. "It gets hard to remember stuff from out there. Maybe that happens when you're all alone. You start forgettin' who you was, an' nothin' you done seem important no more. …The kid was a dealer. Only sixteen. He was gonna kill us. Our gang that wasn't. 'Cause we wouldn't slang rocks for him. An' 'cause we didn't respect him." Robby looked up at the sun again. "Seems stupid now… like, your life can't be much if you gotta kill people just 'cause they don't respect you. But he made a choice… like, pulled the wrong rabbit out of a hat… a big nasty rabbit. …An' maybe I did, too."

30

Jarrett glanced up, but the sun was too bright for his eyes. "Sorry I axed. But, I wish I had homies like yours. My best friend got capped last summer. Now I got nobody."

"You gots your mom."

Jarrett tore the last petal off the flower and threw the skeletal stem away. "Not no more. Not since that fuckin' punk moved in an' got her addicted to shit!" Then he paused. "I almost forgot I killed him last night!" He turned uneasily toward the gates. "Now the cops be huntin' for me."

"How did you kill him?" asked Robby.

Jarrett described what had happened, and Robby listened thoughtfully. Finally he said: "Sound more like a accident. Besides, he was tryin' to kill you, wasn't he? So, what other choice did you have?"

Jarrett dropped his chin to his hands. "No choice at all, but what's that matter? Cops don't listen to kids like me. To them we're all wicked."

"I think we shall tire of that word fairly soon," said Robby as if reciting something. He lay on his back on the slab, his arms crossed under his head, his ragged shirt baring his bronze belly blubber. He gazed at the sky for a minute or two, then shifted his eyes back to Jarrett. "I know it sound kinda preachy, man, but the truth gots a way of comin' out. Like, pushin' up through the bullshit an' lies, like these flowers bustin' the stones. ...You love your mom, don't you?"

Jarrett sighed. "'Course I do. An' she loved me. But, it gotta be hard to love anybody when you hurtin' all the time."

"Maybe you could help her stop hurtin'."

"...How I do that?"

"Maybe you could go back home. Tell her you love her."

"I don't know, man..."

"Don't know what? You gotta be able to say you love her."

Jarrett glanced at the gates again. "I mean take the chance of goin' back after what happen last night."

"Ain't there been times when she helped you?"

"Most of my life, but..."

"Then maybe it time you helped her."

31

Jarrett was quiet for several minutes, hearing the bees and the gentle bird song, lulled by the peaceful trickle of water. Part of him wanted to stay in this place, to rest in the sun and forget his old life and all the shit outside those gates. "But, if I can't do nothin' out there, can I come back here an' stay with you?"

Robby smiled. "I be here, Jarrett." He wiggled out of his dusty shirt. "Take this, bro. You can't wear that bloody ol' rag of yours. People think you a walkin' kid-corpse."

Jarrett looked down at himself again, his arm still a mess, dried blood everywhere. "Guess I do look a little bit dead."

"Only on the outside. C'mon, you can wash in the pond."

The pond was small, about thirty feet wide, and set like a chubby kid's belly button in a soft round tummy of tall green grass. Maybe there had been goldfish once, but they'd probably died of old-age. In the middle of the pond stood a fat naked boy. He was made of bronze, his toes in the water, and holding a vase in his chubby arms. Maybe he was supposed to be Greek, but his hair looked more like an Afro. He and Robby were about the same color... except for some green on the statue. Water trickled out of the vase, like the boy had a job to keep the pond full. Jarrett wouldn't have minded that job here in this place of sunlight and peace. He knelt in the grass at the water's edge to wash his face and wounded arm, then slipped into Robby's old shirt.

"Thanks, Robby. I bring it back."

Robby stretched in the clear morning light, almost losing his jeans. "Take your time." He laughed and spread his arms to the sky. "Maybe I catch me a tan."

Jarrett smiled. As he remembered thinking last night, Robby had sort of a lion-cub look, cuddly under his bushy black mane like a big Pillow Pal for a little kid's bed; a look that invited a hug. Jarrett studied his own reflection mirrored in the water: his muscular body looked menacing, and nobody hugged a panther. He got up and walked to the gates with Robby, unlocked the lock then shook Robby's hand. "I'ma be back tonight, man. Whatever happen out there."

"Don't forget your key," said Robby.

32

SIX

Jarrett closed the gates behind him and locked the padlock. Robby had perched on the mossy tombstone after snagging a book from the grass below. He flipped through the pages, finding his place, then flashed the peace sign. "Later, Jarrett."

Jarrett offered peace in return then headed up the broken sidewalk, passing rows of abandoned houses and boarded-up factory buildings. He stopped at a corner to get his bearings, surprised he'd come so far last night. The street sign was rusty and couldn't be read, but he recognized a water tower looming in the distance. His ribs ached a bit, his wounded arm hurt, and his ankle was throbbing again. He paused to tighten his shoelace, which seemed to help a little.

A few blocks away from the graveyard his stomach let out a plaintive growl when he smelled the aroma of new-born bread. Up the street was a big bakery, a brand that was advertised on TV as being "homemade on the farm every morning." Jarrett didn't see any cows, but delivery vans were coming and going, passing through a gate in a fence. Stacked on a platform in front of the building were so many loaves, pastries and cakes that it took a forklift to move them. Jarrett's last meal had been half a sandwich given to him by a kid at school.

Waiting until a truck arrived and its driver went into the building, Jarrett crept in through the gate and up to the loading dock. He grabbed a box of donuts and ran! His ankle was stabbing pain once more when he finally stopped a block away, but no one seemed to be after him. The donuts tasted like angel food as he limped along

33

the sidewalk.

He passed a little scrap yard, where rusty metal and corpses of cars towered like jagged mountains of junk behind a sagging chain-link fence. A battered old crane like an iron dinosaur was busily feeding a roaring machine that seemed to be able to swallow whole cars and grind them into football-size chunks. It would have been cool to watch for awhile, a kid-thing to do, but Jarrett was checking the street for cops.

A black-and-tan demon came flying at him!

Jarrett stumbled into the trash-filled gutter as a huge dog slammed against the fence, white razor-teeth and hot yellow eyes. The dog continued to snarl and snap as Jarrett slowly backed away. Then came a bellow of laughter, and Jarrett saw a burly white man clad in greasy overalls. The man laughed again as the dog raged at Jarrett, snarling, snapping, dripping drool. It kept lunging against the ancient fence and almost busting through in places where the mesh was patched with wire. The man could see Jarrett was scared, and the dog could pro-bably smell it.

Then, someone jumped down from the rusty old crane... a shaggy-haired white boy of maybe eighteen in boots with steel showing through on the toes. He was shirtless in jeans so soaked with oil they looked like biker leathers. His sun-tanned body was streaked with grime, and his bushy blond hair tumbled over his shoulders beneath a dented aluminum hard-hat. He cursed the dog and gave it a kick. The animal yelped and turned on him, but another dude came running. He was sooty black, also shirtless in jeans, steel-toed boots and battered hard-hat, and packing a long piece of pipe. The dog tucked-tail and fled from the boys, who flung bits of junk at its butt. The man muttered something like "just having fun," but the boys didn't look amused. The blond boy smiled at Jarrett, joined by his sooty companion.

"The boss is a jerk, but he can't help it."

The black boy grinned and added, "Guess his mama done her best with what she had to work with."

The blond boy laughed and high-fived his friend. "An' a dog takes after its master."

The boys were about the same age and build -- lanky, lean-muscled, and equal in height -- and strange as it seemed they might have been twins. This seemed to show most in their faces, as if they shared the same thoughts.

"Um, thanks," said Jarrett, whose heart seemed to hammer his aching ribs. "But I hope you don't get in trouble."

The black boy laughed and twirled the pipe like an iron baton. "The man won't find no other fools to work for the chump-change he pay."

"You cool, little bro?" asked the blond boy.

"Yeah," said the black. He jerked a thumb at the roaring machine. "You look like you been through the shredder."

"I'm okay," said Jarrett. "Um, thanks again." He hurried away before the dudes could really scope him out. The cops were probably looking for him; a dark boy with dreads who'd been beaten up... a wicked boy who'd murdered a man.

Finally nearing his own neighborhood, he cautiously scanned the streets, hiding whenever a car approached. The morning sun seemed to mock his fear, as if nothing bad could happen beneath its friendly glow. He stopped a block away from his house in what must have been the alley he'd stumbled through the night before. There was only a handful of cars up the street, and all were too old and shabby for cops'.

Then he noticed the ancient hearse in the funeral home's weedy driveway. It looked more funny than frightening now, with its bulbous fenders, tons of chrome, and narrow, old-fashioned white-wall tires.

Someone was cutting the weeds in the yard; a slashing shadow as dark as night who swung a savage scythe, something Jarrett had only seen in pictures portraying skeletal Death. But this Grim Reaper was a boy who looked around nineteen, willowy slender and gracefully tall. He wore only jeans and big battered sneaks, his long body shining with silvery sweat as if someone had polished a midnight. Despite his slimness his muscles were hard, though more smoothly sculpted suggesting strength than starkly defined like Jarrett's, and he would have looked fragile if not so tall. His face was almost more

35

pretty than handsome, with high cheekbones, a small snub nose, and full lips at rest in an half-open pout revealing big white teeth. His hair was an ebony dandelion-puff, while his hands and feet looked cartoonishly large, though there was nothing awkward about him. He moved like a stalking cat or a dancer, reaping a harvest of dead yellow thistles with every bright sweep of his deadly blade. He was clearly the long-coated leather-clad shape who'd rolled up in the hearse last night.

If not for the serious shit he was in, Jarrett might have gone over to meet the boy and ask what was up with the old funeral home. Was it going to open for business again? There wasn't a shortage of customers with all the dumb-ass thugs around killing each other to "keep it real," and plenty of rappers encouraging them. The boy seemed too young for an undertaker, but Jarrett didn't have time for questions.

The boy glanced up as Jarrett passed. Their eyes met briefly, but Jarrett was too distracted to smile.

Jarrett stopped in front of his house. The 'hood was almost too quiet. The whispering slash of the slender boy's blade seemed to be the only sound. Maybe this was a trap? The cops could be up in his crib. He recalled again the safety and peace of Robby's sunny grave-yard. Maybe he should go back there? Then, Mrs. Davis came out of the house, dressed in her nurse's uniform. She wouldn't betray him, he'd take the chance.

Mrs. Davis was big and fearless, yet her eyes went wide spotting Jarrett as if she was seeing a ghost. But, leaving the door half open behind her, she came down the steps and gathered Jarrett into her arms.

"Thank God you're alive, son! ...All that blood! ...Nobody knew what happened to you!" She gripped Jarrett's shoulders and studied him. "Lord, you look like you come out a grave! We best get you to the hospital."

But, Jarrett wiggled free. "No. I'm cool. Is my mom all right?"

"Yes, son. She's upstairs. I gave her somethin' to help her rest."

"What about... him?" asked Jarrett.

Mrs. Davis's face went hard. "He won't be causin' you trouble no

36

more. ...Or anyone else this side of a grave."

A shiver ran down Jarrett's spine, even though he'd already known. "I killed him, didn't I?"

Mrs. Davis took Jarrett's shoulders again and carefully searched his eyes. "No you didn't. Listen to me. I saw the whole thing from the top of the stairs. You were defendin' yourself, that's all. Man twice your size! You didn't push him, Jarrett, he fell. His death was no doin' of yours, son. That's God's honest truth, an' I told the cops." Her eyes returned to his wounded arm. "Y'all better come with me."

"No... thanks, Miz Davis. I'ma go up to my mom."

Mrs. Davis hesitated, but finally let go of Jarrett. Reaching into her pocket, she brought out the box-cutter knife. "No reason the cops shoulda found this... was enough splintered wood to done the damage. An' I doubt there be much of an inquest... not for the likes of him. He probably be in the ground by tomorrow."

Mrs. Davis gave Jarrett the blade. "I gotta be goin', son, 'bout to miss my bus." She started down the sidewalk, but paused and turned around. "I work at a rehab center in the evenin's. Here's the address." She pulled a card from her pocket. "You get your mom to come... yes you do. We got nice beds an' comfortable rooms, an' she can stay till she back on her feet."

Jarrett took the card. "Thanks, Miz Davis." He limped up the steps and into the house but stopped at the foot of the stairs. On the floor was an outline in pale white chalk, a child's cartoon of a dead black man. Jarrett had seen them before on the streets. Somehow they always seemed smaller than life, the way a dead spider looked tiny and harmless compared to its frightening shape when alive.

Jarrett felt cold gazing down at the sketch, though the air had been warm when he'd entered the house. The chill seemed to follow him up the stairs as he passed his own blood still bright on the landing. He paused again to study the stains, almost amazed at all he'd lost. But that seemed a little unreal now, like a nightmare remembered in morning sunlight.

Climbing the stairs seemed to warm him again. The apartment door was open. His mother sat on the ragged couch, clad in a bathrobe and fuzzy slippers, her eyes seeking refuge in daytime TV. She turned as Jarrett came in; and he saw that her face was the face he recalled from a long time ago in the past... the mother who'd read those fairytale stories and tucked him into bed at night. He ran to her, awkward because of his ankle, and they hugged for the first time in almost a year.

He sat beside her and held her hand as the TV babbled its own fairytale in a Never Land world of make-believe where people solved all their problems between commercials for wireless phones, fast-food joints and weight loss pills. But, nothing had changed on the real; the door to his room hung splintered and broken. He glanced at the coffee table where a needle and packet of dirty brown powder were only half hidden beneath magazines. The cops must have seen them, but probably hadn't wanted to bother. *Dust to dust*, as the preacher had said when they'd buried Jarrett's homey. All went back to dust when it died.

Yet he'd also said, *sure and certain hope.*

But what was certain about hope?"

"Mom," he said at last. "Miz Davis work at a rehab center." He took out the card. "It just a few blocks from here."

Fear flickered over his mother's face. "Jarrett... honey. You don't understand. It ain't that easy..."

Jarrett let go of his mother's hand. He picked up the needle. He wanted to throw it on the floor and grind it to dust with his sneak. Instead he put it back again, watching his mother's eyes follow. "Dyin' is easy. I wanna help you live. But, you gotta go to that rehab place."

His mother only looked more frightened. "But... if I went there you'd be all alone."

Jarrett shook his head. "I *been* alone, mom. A long time already." He saw the pain his words had caused, and pressed his mother's hand once more. "Got a new friend. Met him last night. Name's Robby. He's cool. So I won't be alone."

"...But, you got school. ...An' there's rent to pay."

Jarrett felt tears try to start, like when he'd stood at the graveyard gates and thought his life was over, but he fought them back and stood up. "You only makin' excuses, mom. You gotta go to the rehab place. It like... well... like, you got a *key*. A key that can let you get out of here... like, out this bad place you got in. But, you gotta use it." He hesitated, still battling tears, then hardened his voice. "I ain't gonna stay here an' watch you die. That be the wickedest thing I could do." He held out his hand. "C'mon an' get ready."

His mother's eyes seemed to clear a little. "Oh, God, son! What happen to you?"

Jarrett knew how dead he looked. "I'm alive, mom. An' so are you. An' we gotta help each other live." He took her hand with a strength that surprised him and helped his mother to her feet.

SEVEN

The rehab center looked haunted, like a mansion in a storybook or the Munsters' house on the old TV show; a big wooden building with turrets and towers and many odd angles and slants to its roof. Its shingles were patched with pieces of tin and its paint was weathered and peeling, but a hand-painted sign in the corner doorway said WELCOME in sunny bright letters.

Mrs. Davis's smile was just as bright as she bustled across the large front room like a tugboat coming to rescue a ship. Jarrett kept hold of his mother's hand, not wanting Mrs. Davis to tow her away. He scan-ned around as they walked to a staircase across a worn but polished floor. He hadn't known what to expect... something like an emergency room of hostile plastic, heartless metal, and merciless glaring white lights. But, despite its shabby exterior the place seemed inviting within. The ancient woodwork was freshly varnished, and the paint on the walls looked new. The building might have once been a hotel, which Jarrett supposed was logical because it was only a few blocks away from the old West Oakland railroad station. The lobby was furnished with couches and chairs; there were tables with magazines, and a TV was tuned to an evening talk show about the war on terror. The handful of people sitting around all looked normal in regular clothes instead of bathrobes or hospital gowns.

To Jarrett, his mom looked brave and cool in a dress she had worn to church on Sundays, though her hand trembled in his. They climbed the stairs to a long hallway, and Mrs. Davis led them on as if she was giving a tour. The passage was lit by candle-shaped bulbs in antique brackets along the walls: they reminded Jarrett of the flower vases in Robby's graveyard house of stone. The rooms were small but newly painted, each with a bed, a chair and a dresser. None of the pieces of furniture matched, but all was well-kept, or at least well-repaired.

Mrs. Davis showed them a room where sunlight streamed in through a west-facing window. Jarrett had carried his mother's things in a little overnight bag. He set it atop the dresser and kissed his mom goodbye.

"I'ma come see you tomorrow," he said, then hesitated, wondering why it seemed so hard to say those three simple words. "I love you," he added.

His mom drew him close in a hug. "I love you, too," she whispered. "My big strong son."

Jarrett didn't feel big or strong, only confused and a little scared. Back in the hall with Mrs. Davis, he pulled out the rag-wrapped needle and the packet of dirty brown powder. "I brung this stuff. Maybe I shoulda flushed it?"

"Pity the toilet." Mrs. Davis took the things with the kind of professional indifference she'd probably give to a shit-filled bedpan. "You done fine, Jarrett. We got a furnace take care of this. Send it right back to hell where it came from."

"Um," Jarrett added. "She wasn't on it real bad. Besides, it ain't very good shi... stuff."

Mrs. Davis patted his shoulder. Your mom gonna be all right, son. She got you, an' she *know* she got you, an' that's more important than anything else."

"Um, it *is* all right, ain't it? Me comin' back tomorrow? ...I seen her hurtin' before."

"Of course you come back. We can help her deal with the physical pain, but what's really important is showin' you love her, bein' there an' givin' her hope."

Jarrett lowered his head. "Don't think I'm very good at that. If I was, she wouldn't be here."

"You done all you could with what you had, so don't go blamin' yourself, son. You can't change the past, what's done is done, but you *can* change the future."

41

Jarrett looked up. "How I do that?"

Mrs. Davis smiled. "The future's kinda like a bus, it's comin' whether you want it or not. You can get on board an' go where you want. Or, you can stand there an' let it go by... in which case you ain't goin' nowhere."

"Buses don't always go where you want."

"But they can usually get you close. ...Now, you come with me an' I fix that arm." Mrs. Davis examined it closely. "Should have had stitches. Gonna leave a big scar."

Jarrett shrugged. "Ain't gonna show much, I'm way too black."

"Well, you a fast healer, I give you that. Just like my boy Randy. Always fallin' off that skateboard of his."

"Randy used to skate?" asked Jarrett. That seemed a little hard to believe, recalling the six-foot mass of muscle who'd rescued him from several beatings.

"'Course, I ain't no fool," Mrs. Davis went on. "Some of his wounds didn't come from skatin', but I always knew he'd beat the streets, an' he's goin' to college after the Army."

"Guess you worry about him a lot, over there fightin' terrorists?"

"Yes I do, an' I pray every night. But terror ain't nothin' new to him, comin' up in this neighborhood. He's got a good head on his shoulders, an' he know when to keep it down."

Mrs. Davis led Jarrett downstairs and they walked along a high-ceilinged hall where cooking aromas flavored the air, making Jarrett's stomach growl. They passed a doorway and he glanced in, seeing a sort of restaurant kitchen with a huge ancient stove, a big metal sink, and a wooden cold-box with shiny brass handles that looked like something out of a morgue. Light bulbs dangled from wires overhead, and pots and pans hung from long iron racks. A big covered kettle of what smelled like gumbo was simmering on the stove.

Then Jarrett saw Robby washing dishes! He stopped at the doorway and stared... but then realized he was seeing a girl. She stood at the sink, her back to Jarrett, busily scrubbing a big frying pan. She wore faded jeans, beat-up sneaks, and a T-shirt that didn't quite cover her middle. The combination of chubbiness, similar clothes, honey-bronze skin and Afroish hair made her look a lot like Robby.

Mrs. Davis led Jarrett on, and unlocked a door to a room that resembled a doctor's office. There was a glass-fronted cabinet with various medicine bottles and jars, and an antique examination table of nickel-plate and worn black leather. Mrs. Davis told Jarrett to take off his shirt and climb on the table, then she bent close to check out his ribs. His midnight skin didn't easily bruise, but she seemed to know where to look for damage.

"Ow!" he said as she prodded him gently and clasped her hands to his lean-muscled sides.

"Take a deep breath for me, son. That hurt?"

"Just... a little."

"More than a little, I'm thinkin'. But, nothin' seem to be busted in there. How's that ankle? I seen you limpin'."

"S'cool."

"Let me be the judge of that." Mrs. Davis removed Jarrett's shoe and wiggled his foot back and forth.

"Ow, dammit!" said Jarrett. "...Sorry." He noticed his sock was full of holes and a toe stuck out cartoonishly.

Mrs. Davis smiled. "I heard a lot worse." She unlocked the medical cabinet and took out a big brown bottle.

Jarrett cocked his head. "What's that stuff?"

"Ol' Doc Tindle's Horse Liniment. This'll take care of your trotters."

"...Oh."

"Take off your sock. This gonna burn a little at first, but it start feelin' better right after."

"Ow!"

Mrs. Davis massaged the stuff into Jarrett's ankle. It smelled like gasoline, burned like hell, and he squirmed on the slippery leather. "That shi... that stuff really for horses?"

"Them, too. Now let's see that arm."

Jarrett jerked his arm away. "You ain't puttin' that nasty ol' shit on my arm!"

Mrs. Davis chuckled. "Got some dog disinfectant for that."

Jarrett rolled his eyes. "Oh, cool."

Mrs. Davis examined his arm. "Still a few pieces of glass in there, I'll have to pick 'em out."

Jarrett tried to maintain his cool as Mrs. Davis armed herself with what looked like an ice-pick and oversize tweezers. He tried to think of something nice -- the tall green grass in the quiet graveyard, the sweet smell of flowers and buzzing of bees -- as Mrs. Davis went to work. She knew what she was all about, and it didn't hurt too much, though Jarrett winced when she probed with the pick. Then he glanced to the hallway door, saw the girl, and bit back an "ow."

It wasn't surprising he'd thought of Robby, seeing the girl in the kitchen. She was rolly-poly chubby, and also about thirteen. Her face was cheerful and button-nosed, with chipmunk cheeks and rosebud lips. Her long-lashed eyes held a hint of gold, and her forehead was shadowed by bushy curls. Her faded black T-shirt was tightly too small and clung to the lush round shapes of her breasts, while her tummy lapped over the top of her jeans and the shirt bared the soft oval cave of her navel.

Jarrett forgot about his arm and whatever Mrs. Davis was doing... sawing it off for all he knew. The girl had been peeping him out. For a second he swore he could feel her eyes. It was almost the same sensation he got when waiting at home for the bathtub to fill, feeling the feathery fingers of steam caressing his naked body. Then the girl said:

"You don't look like a crackhead, too many muscles."

Mrs. Davis plucked a shard of glass from Jarrett's captive arm.

"Ow, DAMMIT! ...I ain't no crackhead!"

The girl smiled. "Maybe that's why you don't look like one."

"Ya think?" snapped Jarrett. The girl was way past cute, but he found himself feeling annoyed by her 'tude.

Mrs. Davis glanced at the girl. "There's some down-to-earth logic." Then she smiled at Jarrett. "This is Martin Hawker. Her mom does most of the cookin' for us, an' Martin helps out here an' there. Martin, this is Jarrett. His mom is stayin' with us for a while."

Jarrett watched the girl's face, alert for a smirk, but her eyes seem-ed more kind than anything else. She came in and offered a hand, warm and soft from washing dishes but also feeling strong for

44

a girl's. She wore what looked like a homemade bracelet; a sort of African-looking thing woven from strips of colored leather. Her gold-tinted eyes were curious now; they lingered a moment on Jarrett's chest, then shifted away to his arm. "Can I help, Mrs. Davis?" she asked.

Mrs. Davis smiled at Jarrett again. "Martin's gonna be a doctor." She turned to the girl. "'Spect your hands be clean enough. An' all lemony-fresh like they say on TV. Y'all go ahead an' finish him up. I got the glass out. Just swab it good an' wrap a loose bandage."

Jarrett tensed as the girl took his arm and gave it a critical scoping. "Shouldn't this get stitches?" she asked, with an eagerness that made him uneasy. "I need the practice," she added.

Jarrett jerked his arm free. "You ain't gonna practice no stitchin' on me!"

Martin grabbed his arm again as if they were playing with something. "But, check it out, Jarrett. It's all opened up. I can see right down through your *Cutis Vera.*"

"So, quit lookin' at my... cutie very."

"You also have a richly pigmented *Rete Mucosum.*"

"Yeah? Then it the only rich thing I got."

Mrs. Davis chuckled. "'Member your beside manner, Martin."

Then, to Jarrett's astonishment, she up and left the room, leaving him alone with the girl, who petted his shoulder soothingly. "There, there."

"Oh shut... hush," growled Jarrett. "Think you Nancy Nurse?"

"That's chauvinistic. Think you a big, bad thugger-boy?"

"That's stereotypical," Jarrett snapped. "'Sides, I seen enough of that shit to last me the rest of my life."

"So have I," said Martin. "Quit wigglin' like a maggot an' let me get to work."

"S'pose if Miz Davis trust you, you ain't gonna kill me."

"You look half dead already."

"Bedside manner."

"You'd make a very handsome corpse."

"Stitchin' ain't all you need practice on." Jarrett relaxed a little. Martin did seem to know about doctoring things as she dabbed at

45

some blood with a cotton swab. "I suppose you don't like fat girls?"

"Huh?" said Jarrett. "I wouldn't call you fat."

"Anorexically-challenged?"

"Huh?" he said again, feeling stupid.

"A rose by any other name..."

"The hell you talkin' about?"

Martin rolled her eyes. "I guess you're a typical G. Readin' gives you a headache, huh?"

"I ain't no dumb-ass G! An' I read a few books when I got time... which ain't been lately. ...Fact is, that rose thing be Shakespeare."

Martin gave Jarrett a new look of interest. "Well, give that boy a cigar. But, I bet you learned it from TV."

"Well... yeah. But, I still know who said it first."

"So, why's your mom stayin' with us?"

"Um, she was on shi... you know. But, not too bad."

"That's hopeful," said Martin, still concentrating on Jarrett's arm. "So, who messed you up?"

"Done it myself tryin' to jump out a window."

Martin shifted her golden gaze to Jarrett's midnight eyes. "Should I ask why?"

Jarrett shrugged. "Don't matter now. It done an' buried... 'least I hope. What important be my mom."

Martin finished cleaning the wound, then got a bandage out of the cabinet. She glanced at the box and giggled a little.

"What's funny?" asked Jarrett.

"It says flesh-colored."

"Oh. Some people don't got as 'richly pigmented a Reet Moo-cow-scum' as me." Jarrett smiled. "I had a box of crayons..."

"Yeah," said Martin. "I had them, too. I used to think peaches were flesh-colored."

Jarrett laughed. "I used to think white people were peach-colored."

Martin glanced at the cabinet. "Most of this medical stuff is old an' the hospital threw it away. New bandages are politically-correct."

Jarrett shrugged. "Politically-correct don't correct nothin', it just makes bad shit sound like it ain't... like callin' a retard mentally-

46

challenged. It's just another hate-word if haters wanna use it that way."

"That's down-to-earth logic," said Martin.

"Might's well call a dead person 'livin' impared.'"

Martin laughed. "That's a good one."

"Um, so, you work here?" asked Jarrett as Martin bandaged his arm.

"After school an' weekends. Mostly I help my mom in the kitchen. This is her second job 'cause she cooks the graveyard shift at Dennys." Martin did a last wrap on the bandage and gently taped it in place. "I'm not supposed to be doing this. It's 'hazardous work' an' against the law."

"If the law say that, then the law is a ass." Jarrett puffed his chest a bit. "That from a Charles Dickens book."

"We had to read that one in school," said Martin. "Here, let me put on your shoe. ...Your ankle's kinda swollen."

"Miz Davis put some horse shi... stuff, on it."

"Smells like shit, don't it?"

"Maybe shit smell different to a horse. Um... so, I guess I should put on my shirt?"

Martin smiled. "Seems like a shame. Like puttin' pajamas on a panther."

Jarrett shrugged. "Clothes supposed to be who you are. Or 'least what you want other people to think."

"That's kinda profound. Like what you said about politically-correct."

"Aw, I just thought it up." Jarrett slipped into his shirt, and Martin helped with his bandaged arm.

"Well," she said. "You don't seem to believe in dress to impress. Is that blood on your jeans... yes it is. An' that shirt's just a rotten ol' rag."

Jarrett frowned. "A friend of mine give me this shirt, an' now he don't even got one. An', you ain't exactly the queen of dope threads."

"Why bother? I'm fat."

"The politically-correct hate word is obese," said Jarrett. "An' I

47

think you look cool. Like, you wouldn't be you if you wasn't."

Martin cocked her head. "That pretty profound, too. I'm savin' my money for stuff that matters. Like goin' to college an' medical school. Why should I dress to impress ghetto fools?"

Jarrett frowned. "That what you think I am?"

"No. Besides, you're not dressed like one. You look like my dad goin' to work. He drives a bulldozer at the dump." She seemed to wait for Jarrett's reaction.

Jarrett only shrugged. "Sound like honest work to me. I be savin' my green for important stuff, too. Like helpin' my mom get back on her feet."

Martin smiled. "Nope, you ain't no G-frontin' fool."

Jarrett sighed. "I be savin' if I had any green. ...Um, so you work here every day?"

"Just about. It's against the law, too... child labor."

"What ain't against the law?" said Jarrett. "My mom used to say they get more an' more laws an' less an' less justice."

"That's also kinda profound."

"Maybe the truth only sound profound 'cause people are used to hearin' lies."

"That's pretty profound all by itself."

"Aw, I just thought it up," said Jarrett, then added, "I'ma come back tomorrow to see my mom. ...Um, maybe I see you, too?"

Martin smiled. "I'll be here."

EIGHT

It was early evening when Jarrett got home. He stripped off Robby's dusty old shirt and shed his raggedy, blood-stained jeans. The day had been warm, but the air in his room seemed strangely cold and a shiver ran through his body. He went to the broken window where a salt-scented breeze sighed in from the bay with an eerie whispering sound... maybe because of the jagged glass fangs. Then he gathered the few other clothes he owned and took them down to the washing machine in the house's crypt-like basement. Like Martin he didn't dress to impress, but that was no reason to wear *dirty* rags.

He came back upstairs defiantly naked, not caring if anyone saw him; though everyone else who lived in the place was safely locked behind their doors. He took a long and much-needed bath, after sealing his bandage in plastic wrap to keep from getting it wet. For the first time in months he felt clean.

He found the only fresh towel in the house and was drying himself when the door buzzer sounded. He froze for a moment... who could it be? The man had done most of his "business" out on the street and in neighborhood bars, though a few desperate marks had found their way here, most of them looking like zombies with eyes like burned-out light bulbs. Jarrett felt a shiver of fear, not wanting to deal with the walking dead, as the buzzer blatted a longer note. But he tied the towel around his waist and padded across the living room, dripping a trail on the floor. At the hallway door he hesitated, his finger on the speaker switch while he thought about running away.

49

To where?

He pictured himself running back to the graveyard in nothing but the towel... which was pink! What would Robby think of him? And, maybe more importantly, what would he think of himself? Still, his finger trembled a bit as he finally flipped the switch. He tried to make his voice sound hard. "Yeah?"

"Jarrett Ross?"

Another shiver ran down Jarrett's spine like the icy touch of a skeleton finger. He'd heard enough cops in his life to know he was hearing one now... and worse, the voice was white. But he tried to chill out. "Yeah?"

The voice from the speaker sounded tired: "Oakland Police. Detective Sergeant Locke. I need to ask you some questions."

Again, Jarrett thought of running away... but how long could he hide? "Miz Davis already talk to you people."

The voice grew cop commanding: "Somebody died in this house last night. Maybe that doesn't mean much around here, but I need a statement from you."

When Jarrett hesitated again, the man threw down his front of politeness. "Look, kid," he warned. "I'm doing you a favor. I could lock you up for questioning. ...Forty-eight hours if I want to. I'm tried, hungry, and I want to go home, so make it easy on both of us."

Jarrett found he was sweating as he tried to force his mind to think. Cops had a way of making you guilty even when you weren't. Did they know he'd sold crack for the man at school? But, they could have busted him months ago... along with fifty other kids.

Finally, and no longer trusting his voice, Jarrett pushed the unlock button. He wished he had something more to wear, and considered a towel of a different color, but heard the cop on the creaky stairs. He took a deep breath, unbolted the door and went to the couch and sat down. The cop didn't knock but came right in; a fortyish man of medium build with ice-blue eyes and sandy blond hair. His jacket was open just enough to keep his gun ready for action. He glanced around the shabby room as if to confirm what he already knew.

"Jarrett Ross?"

"Yeah." Jarrett didn't get up -- he felt naked enough already and no longer defiant about it -- but something made him point to a chair. "You can sit down if you want."

The man seemed to listen for sarcasm, then maybe decide he hadn't heard any. "Thanks." He seated himself on the edge of the chair as if he thought it might have a disease and pulled out a leather-bound notebook. Then he studied Jarrett's bandage. "You all right?"

"Yeah. Miz Davis a nurse."

"I know," said the man. He sat for a moment scanning Jarrett as if he was something to fit in a box and he had lots of boxes.

Jarrett wished he looked like Robby... light-skinned, chubby, and harmlessly cute. The cop probably thought he *could* kill with all his muscles and midnight shade.

"She's your best defense witness," said the man. "Nice lady, too. That probably helps, since she's also your only defense witness."

"She seen the whole thing," said Jarrett.

Detective Locke nodded. "That's what she said. And the Coroner confirmed cause of death: he broke his neck when he fell. ...Or was pushed."

"Fell," said Jarrett.

The man watched Jarrett carefully. "He didn't suffer much."

"Too bad," said Jarrett before he could stop. "He made a lot of people suffer."

"Did you hate him?"

It didn't seem to matter. "Yeah."

The man made a note but nodded. "I would have. Punk had a record. Wife-beater type. Kids too, from the way you look. Originally from St. Louis. ...You know that?"

"We didn't talk," said Jarrett.

"Just 'business?'"

Jarrett shrugged. "You wouldn't understand."

"I won't unless you tell me the truth."

"Um... should I have a lawyer?" asked Jarrett, already regretting whatever he'd said.

"Not unless I arrest you."

51

"So, you might?" asked Jarrett.

The man shrugged. "We'll see how it goes. ...You're entitled to an advocate."

"What's that?" asked Jarrett.

"You don't have to talk to me alone."

"I'm used to bein' alone," said Jarrett. Then he scowled. "Miz Davis call you lots of times when he was beatin' on me an' my mom. An' mostly you never come."

The man made another note in his book. "That works both ways."

"What you sayin'?"

"Gives you a motive."

"...Oh."

"You don't like cops, do you, Jarrett?"

Jarrett met the man's eyes. "You never give me no reason to."

The man might have sighed. "I suppose not. Sometimes I don't like them either."

"So, why you be one?"

"I used to be young, believe it or not. Thought I could change the world. Maybe I let the world change me, but it's something you learn to live with." The man glanced at the coffee table, seeming to note that the packet of powder and needle were gone. "How's your mother?"

"She... visitin' a friend."

Locke shook his head. "I asked *how* she is. I already know where she is." He leveled his eyes at Jarrett. "And a few other things. You don't play sports at school... too 'busy,' I guess... but you look pretty strong. You work out?"

"No, an' I never liked sports," said Jarrett, not knowing what else to say.

"I didn't either," said the man. "Our coach was a bully. I hate bullies. They make themselves stronger by making you weaker."

"Like cops," said Jarrett.

"A few," said the man. He lay the notebook on his knee. "My son's about your age, and he doesn't like cops either. Or sports. Just about lives on his computer. Looks like it, too, if you know what I

52

mean"

"That bother you?" asked Jarrett.

"No," said the man. "Because he's got a brain in his head."

"I mean that he don't like cops," said Jarrett.

Again the man shrugged. "Most people don't, including kids. It's something you learn to live with."

"I can't afford a computer," said Jarrett. "Is that my fault?"

"I suppose not." Surprisingly the man made a note. "Where did you go last night? After the decedent 'fell?'"

"Decedent?" asked Jarrett.

"The dead man."

"I... stayed with a friend."

Another note. "Does your friend have a name?"

"I... don't wanna get him into this."

"All right... for now. Just tell me what happened."

Jarrett did, and told the truth. The detective nodded at everything no matter how it sounded and made a lot of notes. When Jarrett finished, he asked, "You have the box cutter?"

It was in Jarrett's room on the dresser. "I... lost it when I ran away."

The man closed his book. "A smart kid would have." He glanced around the room again as if noting the mess in his mind. "Is there somebody I can call?"

"For what?" asked Jarrett.

"You shouldn't be staying here alone."

"Is that against the law?"

"Yes."

"I'm gonna crib with my friend again."

"I'll buy that for now."

"So, you might arrest me?" asked Jarrett.

"We'll see how it goes." Locke glanced at his watch then got to his feet smiling an unreadable smile. "Don't leave town."

Jarrett bolted the hallway door as Locke descended the stairs. He was feeling guilty of many crimes now, from Murder One to skipping school. He was shiny with sweat and his hands were shaking. He went to the fridge and snagged a forty. A few gulps of malt chilled him out. He'd done all he could with what he had.

He went back down to the basement to put his things in the dryer and found with dismay that Robby's shirt had fallen apart in the wash-ing machine. He thought of the boy with night coming on, then picked out his best shirt to give him. His mother had bought it a year ago at the Salvation Army store, an ancient Steadham skateboard shirt with a smiling dreadlocked skull on the front. Robby seemed to like jokes about death, and the skullish shirt seemed appropriate dope for a kid who cribbed in a graveyard.

The sun was beaming a bloody red glow through the broken window's jagged fangs when Jarrett returned to his room but the air still felt unnaturally cold as breeze whispered in from the dying day. Jarrett started to put on his jeans, but paused as Martin came into his mind. He recalled how she'd looked while tending his arm, her honey-bronze wholeness hardly contained by her tight-clinging T-shirt and ancient Levis. Thinking of Martin warmed him inside. He'd felt the same warmth when she'd bandaged his arm and her chubby thigh had pressed his leg. But then the cold returned.

He went to the window. The sun was setting beyond the bay and the darkening skyline of San Francisco. He noted the ancient truck-sized hearse still parked in the funeral home's driveway. The slim black boy must have worked all day; the weeds were gone from the little front yard and the boards removed from the house's windows. The power must have been restored because light shone out through a deep-purple curtain. A sprinkler was even sparkling to resurrect the long-dead lawn. Night was settling in, but Jarrett saw a slender shape at rest on the shadowy porch steps. The boy was still shirtless in dangerous jeans, the scythe standing against the rail, its blade curving halo-like over his head. He seemed to be sipping a forty; and Jarrett wished he could join him to talk for a while and maybe be friends. But he already had a friend to think of... a friend who might need his help.

He put on his jeans, slipped the box knife in a pocket – he'd lose it somewhere down a sewer drain -- then he went to the kitchen. He gathered the food that remained in the fridge... most of a bucket of Church's chicken, a cardboard tub of potato salad, and part of a loaf

54

of bread. He snagged a forty of Eightball, found two candles in a drawer, packed everything in a garbage bag and added a blanket from his bed. Finally, he put on his sneaks, grabbed his coat and set out for the graveyard.

NINE

It was almost dark when he reached the gates, after trekking though alleys and industrial streets of truck garages and welding shops, all heavily shuttered and barred for the night. The dog had been on patrol in the scrap yard, but Jarrett had passed on the opposite sidewalk, almost sneaking along in the dusk. A guard now stood at the bakery gate, as if donuts and bread were terrorist targets.

The old street lamp had not yet come on, and shadows shrouded the weedy sidewalk along the cemetery wall. Jarrett peered in through the rusty bars and saw with surprise that Robby was perched on the mossy tombstone exactly where he'd been that morning and seem-ingly lost in his book.

"Yo, man!" called Jarrett. "You catch your death sittin' out there with no shirt!"

Robby hopped down, stashed his book in the grass, and came to the gates with a grin. "Never was much good at runnin' so death got a good chance of gettin' away. An', like I said, I'm used to the cold. ...I did say that, didn't I?"

"Yeah." Jarrett unlocked the lock with his key. "Brung us some food an' a forty."

Robby giggled. "Party time in da boneyard!" He watched as Jarrett relocked the chain, then asked, "What happen out there today?"

"First put this on." Jarrett gave Robby the Steadham shirt. "Your old one croaked in the wash, sorry."

"This is cool," said Robby. "I used to have one like this."

"Oh yeah," said Jarrett. "You told me you skated."

"Did I?"

"When you was fixin' my ankle last night."

"Oh, yeah. Is it fixed?"

"Still hurts but it works."

Robby put on the shirt. "Thanks, I feel warmer already. But, what you do today?"

Jarrett explained about his mom as they walked up the path to the little stone house, pushing their way through the tangled weeds.

"That was a cool thing to do," said Robby. "Wish I coulda done that for my mom. But, what about the cops?"

"Guess I'm under suspicion," said Jarrett. "But I feel like I always been under suspicion ever since I was born."

He paused on the crypt's vine-shrouded porch. "Met a girl at the center today. Name's Martin." He smiled. "Kinda chubby... well, more than kinda. She remind me of you. Not just how she look, but more how she think. ...You don't got a sister, do you?"

"Not that I know of." Robby grinned and patted his chest. "She got these as cool as mine?"

Jarrett smiled. "I didn't get to see 'em like yours, but under her shirt they look awesome. ...But I mean like just part of her y'know? Like, the whole package is awesome, includin' bein' smart."

"'Course," said Robby. "'Cause it the whole person that count, not just what's on the outside. That's gonna get old an' die someday, but inside is forever."

"That's pretty profound," said Jarrett.

"Aw, I just thought it up."

"You ever think about girls, Robby?"

"Nah, I just think about ghouls."

Jarrett made a face, but then touched Robby's shoulder. "You could come home with me tomorrow. Crib at my place. I'm alone till mom gets out of rehab."

"...I kinda got used to it here," said Robby.

Jarrett looked around. Night had fallen and stars shone above. The tombstones and statues stood silent and pale, and the pond was a shimmering, silver-black mirror. "This place is pretty cool... for a grave-yard... but like I axed you this mornin', don't you get lonely some-times?"

"Sometimes," said Robby. "But, I forget stuff. Like, I almost forgot bein' lonely till you showed up last night."

"You scared of goin' outside 'cause the cops might be lookin' for you?"

"Lookin' for me?" asked Robby.

"'Cause of what you did, man. You an' your friends... the gang that wasn't. When you had to cap that dealer. Don't tell me you forgot."

"Oh, that," said Robby. "Nah, I'm waitin' for Eric. ...I told you 'bout him, didn't I?"

"Yeah," said Jarrett. He pulled out the forty and offered it.

"Cool!" Robby poured a little onto the ground. "For all the dead homies who been forgot." Then he took a gulp and burped. "Ain't had no malt since Eric here last. I almost forgot what it tasted like."

"Um?" said Jarrett. "'Scuse me for axin', but, you gots a learnin' disorder?"

"Nah, I just forget stuff. I was dropped on my head when I was a baby. My skull's a little flat on top."

"You told me that already."

Robby returned the bottle. "Ain't like I didn't warn you."

Jarrett took a couple of swigs before pulling open the iron door to the narrow width allowed by its chain. "Damn!" he said, peering into the dark. "I forgot to bring matches."

Robby dug in his pocket. "You can have these."

Jarrett took the little box. "I seen this kind in K-Mart. They come from Australia. Supposed to be waterproof, huh?"

"They don't work underwater," said Robby. "But they light in the rain. Or if you drop 'em in the toilet. ... 'Course, you might not wanna touch 'em then."

Jarrett lit one of the candles he'd brought, then shed his coat and squeezed through the doorway. The pale white marble reflected the flame, and the little brass vases and heavy slab handles glimmered like gold in the flickering light. He put the candle in the old forty bottle, then spread out his blanket and unpacked the food. Robby sat down with his back to a slab, and they ate with their fingers while

58

sharing the malt. Robby did most of the eating and drinking but Jarrett didn't mind: he'd eaten so little in the last few months that it didn't take much to fill his stomach. He noted again the names and dates carved in the slabs that lined the walls. Then he pointed to the slab behind Robby's back. "How come there ain't no name on that one?"

Robby shrugged. 'Guess whoever this place belong to ain't had nobody die in a while."

Jarrett read the dates on the other slabs. "That one up there say 1882 to 1943. An' it's the newest. Somebody else should have died by now."

Robby passed back the near-empty bottle. "Maybe the whole family's dead."

Jarrett studied the nameless slab. "It ain't cemented shut like the others."

"Yeah." Robby knocked on the dusty stone, making an eerie hollow sound. "It pull open like a drawer."

"You opened it?" asked Jarrett.

"Nah," said Robby. "Takes a lot more muscle than I got. But my homies opened it once."

"Why?" asked Jarrett.

Robby shrugged again. "Seemed like a cool idea at the time. We used to come here an' hang. Kids need a place where there ain't no shit."

"Yeah," agreed Jarrett. "But places like that are hard to find." He passed back the bottle. "Guess Donny couldn't come with you 'cause he was too fat to climb over the gates. An' even if he could, a fat kid couldn't get through that door."

"Did I tell you 'bout Donny?"

"Duh."

Robby smiled. "Nothin' bothered Donny much." He waved a hand toward the door. Even all the shit out there. Like, bein' fat gave him time to think instead of doin' dumb-ass shit."

"But, comin' here wasn't dumb," said Jarrett.

Robby's face saddened. "I was thinkin' about other shit."

"Oh," said Jarrett. "Mean what happened... killin' that kid?"

59

Robby sighed. "Maybe someday I forget that, too." He tilted the bottle and drank the remains, then lay back against the slab and patted his belly. "Ain't been this full since I can't remember. Not since the back days with Donny. ...Donny, Randers, Whitey an' Weasel." He thought for a moment. "Oh, an' there was Kevin, too."

"What were they like?" asked Jarrett.

Robby seemed to search his mind, as if calling up his friends one by one. "Kevin was kinda lean an' mean with his muscles showin' like his skin was too tight. Kinda like you, 'cept not as much. Randers was totally ripped, even more muscles than you. Weasel was just about average, an' Whitey had lots of chub like me."

"Whitey?" asked Jarrett. "You had a white dude in your gang? Even if it wasn't a gang."

"Whitey was black."

"So, why...?"

"It was his street name," said Robby. "But Weasel an' Kevin were white. All those dudes come up together. ...Funny, I forgot about that... Weasel an' Kevin bein' white. If people are good their color don't matter."

"I found that out today," said Jarrett. "A white boy saved my ass this mornin'."

"How that happen?"

"A junkyard dog come after me when I was walkin' home. I always been sorta scared of dogs 'cause a pit bull bit me when I was eight." Jarrett pulled up his shirt. "See? The scars you get when you're little never seem to go away. I'd like to forget some things like you do."

Robby sighed. "But I forget the good things, too."

"What was Eric like?" asked Jarrett.

"Black as a panther like you, but without all his muscles showin'. Like, slim without bein' skinny but way stronger than he looked. He was in another gang but he did whatever he wanted an' nobody messed with him."

"'Cause he had a gun?" asked Jarrett.

"Yeah. But he didn't need it much 'cause he was a magic voodoo werewoof boy... you'll see what I mean if you meet him. He could

60

probably open this slab by sayin' some magic words."

Jarrett regarded the blank marble slab. "You could probably open it... like if you had a crowbar or somethin'. If I'd died last night, you coulda put me in there."

Robby looked surprised. "Why?"

"Save my mom the cost of a coffin, an' a funeral with nobody there." Jarrett looked around. "This place feels safe to me... even with skeletons all around. I would of liked it better in here than where they buried my homey. That place was a dead-people's project." He smiled. "An' you could of read me ghost stories like Eric done for you."

"I wouldn't wanna scare you, even if you were dead."

Jarrett settled against the wall, then glanced at the stack of dusty old books. "You read all those?"

"A zillion times. 'Course I know 'em all by heart, even if I forget I do. That big black one is all about magic, *The Seventh Book Of Moses.*"

"Looks like a Bible," said Jarrett. "My mom used to take me to church... before she stopped believin' I guess."

"There's a Bible in the pile," said Robby.

"Ain't that sorta strange?" asked Jarrett. "The Bible an' magic books together?"

"Why? They say the same things about doin' good stuff. Only in different ways." Robby picked up the Bible. "Lotta magic in here, too. 'Course, most people don't understand it. You know the word, 'gospel?' It really be short for God's spell."

Jarrett yawned, growing sleepy. "Mean God could pull rabbits out hats?"

"If He can bring the dead back to life, pullin' a rabbit ain't shit."

"I never thought about that."

"Here's another book about magic." Robby snagged a heavy volume bound in dark brown leather. He blew off the dust. "Lotta cool stuff in here, too. ...How 'bout some Cephalonomancy?"

Jarrett yawned again. "What's that?"

"Fortune-tellin' by boilin' a ass's head."

"...What?"

61

"Ass is a old word for donkey. It's right there in the Bible." Robby picked up and paged through the Bible. "See? Ass. People rode asses before they had cars. Even Jesus rode an ass. An' this warrior dude... I think he was Jewish... slayed a whole army with nothin' but the jawbone of a ass."

"Guess that was before they had guns," said Jarrett.

"Yeah," said Robby. "Guns make slayin' so easy even a kid can do it."

"Could you read me somethin' about magic?" asked Jarrett.

Robby picked up *The Seventh Book Of Moses*. "How about callin' up ghosts?"

Jarrett looked at the long stone slabs. "You ain't really gonna do that, are you?"

"Nah. You only supposed to call up a ghost when you really need their help. Otherwise they get pissed."

"...Well... maybe one of them comics instead."

"How 'bout his one; *Tales From The Crypt?*"

"I think that be safer," said Jarrett. "Like, what if you read some magic words an' called up a ghost by accident? Magic sounds like serious shit, an' them ain't rabbit bones in here!"

Robby opened the comic book. "'It was a dark an' stormy night.'"

TEN

Jarrett woke up to another rainbow. The stone floor was hard beneath his blanket, yet he felt rested and stronger than yesterday as he sat up and yawned. He looked around the cobwebby crypt in the window's colorful glow but wasn't surprised to find Robby gone. Robby had to be scoring food somewhere, and maybe he went out just before dawn to keep from being seen by cops?

Jarrett sat for a while in the rainbow light, which reminded him of that song about Oz. The birdsong and buzzing of bees outside could hardly be heard through the thick stone walls. He realized this was the quietest place he'd ever been in his life. Was there anywhere left in the world, he wondered, where kids could rest in peace? Where teachers and TV, music and movies, weren't pushing and shoving at you all the time, trying to make you something you weren't, like changing your outside for other people until you forgot your own inside. Was he locked in this city for life, he wondered -- *don't leave town*, Locke had warned -- or, could he use his key to escape?

The air in the crypt was cool from the night, and he thought of the sunshine outside. He saw the remains of the food he'd brought and wondered about his own breakfast. But he wasn't hungry yet, and it would feel good to take off his shirt and warm his bones in the sun.

He got up and tested his ankle, which seemed to be better today. Then he snagged his coat, turned his key, and shouldered open the rusty door to the width allowed by its chain.

63

Everything looked exactly the same as when he'd come out the morning before; soft sunny peace in this place of the dead, and the city seemingly only half real beyond the crumbling mossy-bricked walls. Slipping the key back in his pocket, he stepped from the porch into knee-high grass. He lay down his coat, stripped off his shirt, and shook back his long shaggy dreads. On impulse he took off his shoes and socks. He suddenly wanted to run through the grass, leap over gravestones and dance upon tombs. He almost did, but caught himself... that was something a kid would do.

Leaving his things on the vine-covered porch, he waded his way through the sweet-smelling grass to mount a tomb slab overlooked by an angel. Smiling, he lay down on his back, folded his hands on his chest, and closed his eyes to the golden sunlight.

"Yo."

Jarrett raised up on an elbow. The grin on Robby's chubby face mirrored the smile of the Rasta skull on the front of the ancient skater shirt. Robby plopped down beside Jarrett, a kneecap poking out of his jeans like a poor black kid in an old cartoon. The electrical tape on the toes of his sneaks completed the picture of poverty.

"Don't practice bein' dead," said Robby. "We all be doin' that King Tut lean, an' some of us sooner than later, so keep your ass vertical 'long as you can. Eric read me somethin' one time... 'The grave is a fine an' private place, but none I think do there embrace.' That Shakespere. He's dead."

"Duh," said Jarrett. "So, what's that mean?" He lay down again anyhow.

"Means, dead folks don't get no lovin'," said Robby. "No huggin' or kissin' neither. No laughin', or playin' video games. Or layin' around on your ass in the sun." He leaned over Jarrett and ruffled his dreads. "Yo, Jarrett! No burgers an' fries, no mornin' cartoons, no music or hangin' with homies." He bent close and called into Jarrett's ear. "Hellll-oooo in that skull! You hearin' me?"

But Jarrett broke out laughing. He hadn't laughed in so many months it seemed he'd almost forgotten how. He rose up and grabbed hold of Robby. They tumbled off the mossy slab into the long green grass. Robby wiggled free of Jarrett, surprisingly strong despite

64

all his chub.

"Ooooo!" he giggled, getting up. "You think you a panther with all them muscles? Well, I'm a big fat lion, man, an' I got this fat by eatin' panthers!" He flung himself on top of Jarrett, whuffing out Jarrett's breath with his weight. Jarrett squirmed free and scrambled up. Laugh-ing again, he ran away, darting among the tombstones with Robby in pursuit. They tore through the flowers like mowing machines, dodged around angels, past little stone houses, leaped over graves and bull-dozed the weeds. Robby was faster than his rolly shape promised, and even though nearly losing his jeans, he brought Jarrett down with a flying tackle at the edge of the lily-filled pond.

At last they lay panting side by side atop the grassy mound of a grave. Maybe it was only the sun, or the scent of flowers and green growing things, but Jarrett felt a warmth spreading through him, just as he'd felt in his room yesterday when thinking of Martin Hawker.

"Wanna go for a swim?" asked Robby.

"Yeah!" said Jarrett.

They stripped off their clothes and jumped in the pond, while the fat water-boy with his vase seemed to grin.

Robby splashed Jarrett, who splashed him back. They locked in combat like wrestlers, kicking up waves and water lilies while trying to dunk each other. Finally, gleaming and slippery as seals, they came out to lay on the grave again.

Jarrett brushed back his dripping locks. "I heard you," he said. "About stayin' vertical." He glanced toward the gates. "I know I got stuff need doin' out there, but I ain't played like this in a hella long time. I thought I even forgot how to play." Then he went on a little shyly, "Or what it feels like to touch somebody. ...To... *feel* some-body, I guess what I sayin'." He lay a hand on Robby's chest. "Some-body warm an' real like you."

He felt shy again and took his hand away. "My mom used to hug me a lot. But then she didn't, after... well, after she stopped believin' in whatever you s'posed to believe in."

"My mom hugged me, too," said Robby. "You don't know how much you miss gettin' hugged till you don't no more."

"Um...?" asked Jarrett. "Wanna? Like, there nobody left to hug us

65

but us."

Robby smiled. "You mean like embrace in the grave?"

"Technically we *on* a grave."

The boys sat up, awkward at first, but held each other close a long time, chest to chest and cheek to cheek. Finally Robby sighed. "I forgot how good that feels."

"I almost did, too," said Jarrett.

They lay down in the grass again and Jarrett picked a flower, maybe a daisy or poppy, though he'd never known much about flowers... or cared. "I never done a lot of those things you was sayin' dead people don't do, so how can you miss what you never had?"

Robby thought for a moment, gazing up at the sun. "Maybe that's why a lot of kids think they ain't scared of dyin'. Like, they figure there's nothin' worth livin' for."

Jarrett was still regarding the flower. "When you got nothin', there's nothin' to lose."

Robby shook his head. "You gots your *life* to lose, man. An' believe it or not, that's somethin' real good."

Jarrett's jeans were lying nearby, and he pulled the skeleton key from a pocket. He studied both it and the flower, then popped the flower in Robby's navel and dropped the key in the grass. "But, what about your life, Robby? Don't sound like your homies come 'round much no more. Maybe it's time you got vertical. ...Like, went out an' got on a bus."

"A bus to where?" asked Robby.

Jarrett spread his arms to the sky. "To anywhere you wanna go. Like, think about your future, man. You can't just stay here an' let it go by."

Robby sighed. "I told you I'm waitin' for Eric. ...I *did*...?"

"Yeah you did," said Jarrett. "But..."

"Let's talk about you," said Robby. "I know all about me, an' more than I wanna sometimes. Didn't you say you met a girl?"

"Yeah," said Jarrett. "But, I don't know much about girls. I just started thinkin' about 'em last year... seriously, I mean... an' then the man moved in." Jarrett scowled. "Then there was nothin' to think about 'cept what he was doin' to me an' my mom. ...It was like he

66

done somethin' wicked to me, an' it wasn't just gettin' beat up. He made *me* feel wicked. ...Like, guilty of somethin'. Never had time for girls after that."

Robby smiled. "But now you do."

Jarrett frowned. "I ain't sure. Seem like I gone from wicked to worse. Before, I was only a crack-dealin' punk, but now I'm a thug who murdered somebody."

"Did the cop say that?" asked Robby.

"Probably what he was thinkin'." Jarrett glanced to the gates. "I'm tired of all the shit out there, Robby, I just wanna rest a while. It shouldn't hurt to be a kid."

Robby snorted. "Sound like somethin' Elmo would say. It *does* hurt to be a kid, it even *has* to hurt sometimes 'cause if you can't learn to deal with hurt now, how you gonna deal with it later?"

"Just give me some time to rest," said Jarrett. "Before I have to hurt again."

Time went on to the humming of bees and the soft liquid music of trickling water. Robby fired a cigarette and passed it over to Jarrett. Jarrett took a casual hit; he didn't smoke much, not even weed, but he'd fronted enough to come cool about it. Yet he coughed and made a face. "You dig these out of a coffin?"

"Guess they are kinda old," said Robby. "Like everything else in here." He looked up at the sun. "Except that, it's new every day."

"No it ain't. It the same ol' sun."

"Depend on how you look at it."

"You tryin' to tell me somethin'?" asked Jarrett.

"*You're* new every day," said Robby. "Like, born again every mornin'."

Jarrett frowned. "Feel more like I die every night."

"It's morning now," said Robby. "So it's time to come back to life, even if it hurts. You gonna see your mom, ain't you? An' five to one your crib's a mess. You *was* gonna have it all cleaned up for when your mom comes home?"

"...'Course," said Jarrett.

"An', what about payin' the rent till she get back on her feet? You gonna go back to slangin' rocks?"

"I die before I do that again!"

"An' what about school?"

"It Saturday."

"Every day's Saturday in here."

"Sound cool to me."

"So does havin' ice cream an' cake... unless that's all you got to eat for breakfast, lunch an' dinner." Robby picked up the skeleton key from the grass and lay it on Jarrett's chest. "Check out what it can open for you besides the gates to a graveyard."

Jarrett pocketed the key. "Can I come back tonight?"

Robby smiled. "I be here."

Jarrett got up and put on his jeans, then laughed as Robby walked away. "Gonna put your clothes back on?"

"Oh, I forgot."

Jarrett picked up Robby's shirt. "Don't forget this when the sun goes down."

"I just remembered somethin'," said Robby as they walked to the crypt to get Jarrett's things. "Can you skate?"

Jarrett sat on the step to tie his sneaks. "Used to have a board, but I sold it for food."

Robby vanished into the blackberry vines that overgrew the little stone house, then reappeared with a battered skateboard. "Here, doggie-bro."

Jarrett checked the old plank. Except for dust it looked ready to shred, with cool Indy trucks, Saber-Tooth ribs, and black Bullet Santa Cruz wheels. But he stared at the graphic in sudden surprise... a grinning, dreadlocked Rasta skull like the one on Robby's shirt. "This a ol' Steve Steadham! He was one of the first black skaters. They ain't made these in a million years. Where you get it?"

"Just dug it up."

"I hope that's a joke."

Robby shrugged. "Some kid musta lost it a long time ago."

"But, don't you need it?" asked Jarrett.

"You need it more than me. Ain't no bus, but it's still a ride."

ELEVEN

The morning sun felt just as warm outside the graveyard gates as Jarrett locked the padlock and flashed peace to Robby, who'd recovered his book from the grass and mounted the mossy tomb-stone. But the city's sounds were loud and harsh, its outlines stark and hard. If birds were singing he couldn't hear them, and there weren't any flowers among the weeds that lined the shabby street. Jarrett left his shirt off, tying it around his waist and slinging his coat over a shoulder. He decked Robby's board and rolled up the sidewalk, dodging the worst of the cracks and holes. It had been a year since he'd skated but he found he hadn't lost his skill, and the ancient Steadham cruised like a dream. Despite all the running and wrestling with Robby, his arm and ankle didn't hurt much, and he felt pretty good as he rattled along past the boarded-up houses and dead factories.

But, his stomach was growling with hunger as he neared the commercial bakery and scented new-born bread. The gate wasn't guarded by day, and he watched the vans rolling in, noting how long it took the drivers to load their trucks at the dock. Then they went into the building and returned a few minutes later with what might have been their delivery schedules. At last, when there was no one in sight, he left his coat and the board near the gate and darted to the loading dock. Donuts again would taste really good, but bread would make him stronger. He was going to need all the strength he could find to live in the weeks ahead. He spotted a stack of whole-wheat loaves near the open back doors of a van. Creeping close, he reached for one...

69

A hand shot out and grabbed his wrist!

It was like a horror movie where a corpse popped out of a coffin! Jarrett almost screamed. He frantically fought to free himself, but the hand held on like a pit-bull bite. Then a voice ordered, "Chill out!"

Jarrett stopped his struggles. An older boy, around nineteen, got out of the truck. He was wiry like a junkyard dog, and wore white trousers and matching shirt like tough kids wore school uniforms. His dark-blond hair was shoulder-length, and his indigo eyes, though wary, regarded Jarrett without any anger.

"What you all about?" he demanded. "...You try an' kick me, you'll wish you was dead!"

Jarrett had almost tried. "Wish that now!" he snarled.

The older boy's eyes seemed to read Jarrett's life, and his hard face softened a little. "We all do sometimes." He flicked a glance to the loading dock as a forklift carrying cream-filled cakes rumbled out of the building. "Let's talk." He towed Jarrett around to the side of the truck out of sight of the forklift's driver. "You hungry?"

Jarrett snorted. "I be tryin' to boost some bread if I wasn't?"

The boy gave Jarrett the ghost of a smile. "You already cost me a box of donuts. ...I'm gonna let go. Run away like a rat if you wanna stay hungry."

"They feed you in prison!" snapped Jarrett.

"Not very good. I been there, bro."

"...Oh," said Jarrett.

The boy released Jarrett's wrist. Jarrett poised for a moment, ready to bust for the gates, but then puffed his chest and stood proud. His midnight eyes met the blue ones straight-on. "What did you do?"

The boy shrugged. "Somethin' stupid like this." He smiled a little again. "In case you ain't got the word yet, they don't 'rehabilitate' kids in prison. They just teach you how to be a prisoner."

"So, how come you out?" said Jarrett.

"I didn't believe what they tried to teach me."

"...You gonna give me some bread?"

The boy shrugged again. "They haul more bread to the dump in a day than you ever ate in your life. But, you boost off my truck, it

70

comes out of my pay 'cause I got to account for everything. An' 'course they watch me twice as close 'cause I got a record."

Jarrett lowered his eyes. "Sorry."

The boy studied Jarrett again, and Jarrett recalled Detective Locke who'd looked like he'd heard every lie in the world.

"Word," said the boy. "The only stupid questions are the ones you *think* you're too smart to ask. Nobody I know got sent to prison for askin' any questions, but there's lots of kids locked up behind bars 'cause they thought they knew all the answers." He glanced at his cheap plastic watch. "I gotta get busy, but listen up. Go around to the back of the building. You'll see a brother runnin' a loader. ...A *big* brother. Tell him you're hungry, he can relate. ...But, nobody's gonna feel sorry for you if you're busted crackin' these trucks."

"...Thanks," said Jarrett.

The boy climbed into the van. "One more fact of life, little man; there's always good people around somewhere, an' sometimes they show up when you need 'em."

"Thanks," said Jarrett again. He walked around to the side of the building and found a narrow alley. Fans were humming high on the walls, and the bakery smells were a tempting torture. He flattened himself against the bricks as a dump truck rumbled past. Its bed was covered with canvas, but the scent that trailed behind in the air made Jarrett gape in disbelief... there was *food* being treated like trash!

He hurried on to the rear of the building, but there he stopped to stare again. Ahead was a small paved area about the size of a basketball court and guarded by a chain-link fence with razor wire on top. Another dump truck waited. A construction loader trundled up and dumped what looked like a ton of pies into the back of the truck! Jarrett watched in amazement, but then his eyes went to the loader's driver... it had to be the "big brother." In fact, he was the *biggest* brother Jarrett had ever seen!

The dude was somewhere around nineteen, but his chubby round face and wild bushy hair made him look a few years younger. He was clad in ragged Levis that looked about to bust their seams upon his massive thighs. His chest was a pair of chocolate melons exploding out of a sweaty wife-beater that couldn't even begin to

71

cover the gigantic mass of his belly.

The titanic fat boy drove his machine to a loading dock at the rear of the building where mountains of bread and pastry were piled. He set the loader's parking brake and lowered his blubbery bulk to the ground in a rolly cascade of wobbling fat. His belly hung nearly down to his knees, and his bottom, half bare in the ragged old jeans resembled a pair of planets colliding. It seemed amazing he could walk, yet he moved with a kind of lumbering grace like a bulldozer going somewhere. Puffing his way to the platform, he began tossing bakery things into the loader's bucket.

The dude's awesome size was intimidating, but the food smells tugged at Jarrett's stomach. Shyly, he approached the huge boy. "Um?"

The boy swung around like the junkyard crane. "Whattup?"

"Um..." said Jarrett. "This truck driver 'round in front said you might give me somethin' to eat?"

The huge boy smiled. "What's on your menu?"

"Um, bread?" asked Jarrett.

"Sure. What you want? White, wheat, rye, raisin, oatmeal, seven-grain, nutberry crunch? I don't recommend the Diet Delight."

"It don't matter."

The boy studied Jarrett like the truck driver had. "I can see where you comin' from, bro. A few more pounds wouldn't hurt you. All that muscle without no mass make you look like an artist's anatomy model. C'mon inside." He ponderously climbed the steps to the dock.

"Guess all this stuff ain't no good?" asked Jarrett, following the enormous boy while scanning the huge pile of pastries.

The boy snagged a twin-pack of cream-filled cupcakes, tore it open, popped one in his mouth and offered the other to Jarrett. "A little dry. What you think?"

Jarrett downed the cake in three ravenous bites. "Cool with me."

The fat boy laughed, which looked like an earthquake in chocolate pudding. "Just about anything's good when you're hungry. But they outlived their sell-by date."

"That all that's wrong with 'em?" asked Jarrett. "That don't bother me."

The boy slapped his belly, which rippled in waves. "Never bothered me neither."

"Damn!" said Jarrett. "You got the best job in the world, man! ...Um, need any help?"

The fat boy chuckled. "Wanna look like me?"

Jarrett patted his six-pack. "I could use a few pounds like you said. ...But, guess I ain't old enough, huh?"

"So says the law." The boy squeezed his bulk through a doorway into a room with a desk and chair. His vast body seemed to fill the small space and darken the light all around. "Hang a minute, I get you a sampler. ...Sure you don't got no requests?"

"Whatever be cool."

"I give you enough for a week." The boy squeezed his mass through another doorway while Jarrett scanned the little room. A blaster softly bumped on a shelf, playing the old-school station. There were colored pencils and pens on the desk, along with a big drawing pad. Curious, Jarrett went over to peep. The pages were filled with drawings of kids, some standing alone, some hanging together, others skateboarding or doing stuff like playing vid games or watching TV. Even though they were only cartoons they still looked like on the real kids... fat, skinny, average, muscular, short, tall, light and dark.

Jarrett turned the pages in wonder. Then he looked up, feeling guilty, as the fat boy puffed in with a big cardboard box.

"Sorry for snoopin'," said Jarrett. "But, you done these? They kickin' cool!"

The boy smiled as if Jarrett's opinion was really worth something to him. "You like 'em?"

"Hell yeah, man! They on the real! I *seen* kids like these!"

"Thanks," said the boy. "Sold a few to magazines an' some sites on the web. But, it don't pay much. Why I got this job. But, I wanna do a comic book, an' maybe even a movie someday... animated y'know?"

"That be cool!" said Jarrett. "I never seen nothin' like that before. With black kids, what I sayin', an' just as good as Disney stuff."

"Thanks," said the fat boy again. He handed Jarrett the big box of things... pies and cakes, bread and donuts. "I let you out the back gate. They don't want me givin' this stuff away."

"Why not?" asked Jarrett. "If it goin' to the dump."

"The law says it ain't fit to eat. 'Least not if you're an American." The fat boy grinned. "Guess that make me a terrorist, huh?"

Jarrett sighed. "Sometimes I think I was born one."

"I feel you, man, I come up around here. Y'all come back when you're hungry again."

"Thanks," said Jarrett. "Can I check out some more of your drawin's, too?"

"Sure, dawg. I even make you into one. You got just the look for a panther-boy with mutant magical powers."

"Mean like in the *Thundercats?*"

The fat boy nodded. "I was thinkin' about a new animorph hero."

"Well," said Jarrett, "I ain't no hero, but I could pose."

"I can't pay you."

"That's cool. I just like to be a cartoon."

"I can do a quick sketch if you got the time."

"Sure," said Jarrett. "Want me to flex?"

The fat boy laughed. "You're flexed enough already. Just put down the box an' look out the window. Think magic thoughts." The boy squeezed his bulk behind the desk and picked up a well-chewed pencil. He might not have been very fast on his feet, but he made the pencil draw like the wind.

Jarrett tried to think magical things, and remembered Robby's dusty old books. Then he had a new thought and asked, "You give food to other kids? Like a dude about as old as me? Honey-brown an' real chubby. Kinda... well, cute. Like a fat lion cub. Gots a 'fro an' giggles a lot."

The fat boy seemed to think for a moment, but then shook his head. "Used to know a dude like that when I was about your age." He shrugged. "But things are different now. There's a few hungry kids come 'round every week, but they all skinny an' don't laugh much." He put down his pencil. "Here you are."

"Already?" asked Jarrett, taking the paper.

"Time warps fast when you're havin' fun."

Jarrett studied the pencil cartoon. He was glad he was too dark to show a blush because the young figure was freezerburn cool, with powerful shoulders and paving-stone chest. But he *was* a mutant panther-boy, with proud pointed ears and a long graceful tail. He stood on a cliff surveying a jungle and holding a long slender spear. "Damn!" he said.

"It was just a quick sketch."

"No, man! It ROCKS! I wish I looked like this on the real!"

The fat boy smiled. "The tail could be a problem in social situations."

"Not the way you drew it! Almost wish I had one!"

The fat boy smiled again. "Maybe you do look like that. Somewhere."

Jarrett glanced behind himself, almost expecting to *see* a tail... the fat boy's drawing was really that good. "Huh?"

"There's a saying in sci-fi: 'the universe is big enough for anything.'"

"Never read much of that," said Jarrett.

"A lot of kids don't read anymore... 'least until they get locked up. But, I read a lot when I was your age." The fat boy patted his mammoth belly. "I was built for a dreamer instead of a doer."

"Nah," said Jarrett. "You done a lot, man. Just lookin' at this make me feel really good."

"That's what cartoons supposed to do."

"...Um, could I have it?"

"'Course. It's you."

"Thanks, man. Thanks a lot!" Jarrett held out his hand. "I'm Jarrett."

"Double-D," said the fat boy, doing the brother-shake with Jarrett.

"'Cause of the Ed, Edd an' Eddy cartoon? An' 'cause Double-D is smart?"

"Nah. 'Cause I'm twice the size of most other dudes."

Jarrett scanned the sketch again. "But, don't you need this for drawin' more?"

75

Double-D chuckled. "You're livin' in my head now. I'll call you back whenever I need you. Besides, I never forget a tail."

TWELVE

The bakery box was so full of food that Jarrett walked home with the skateboard on top and ate six donuts on the way. He'd kept a careful watch for cops, and had hidden whenever a cruiser appeared. He was also sure he'd seen the detective parked at the curb in a rat-colored car a few doors up the street from his house.

He locked the apartment door behind him, set the box on the coffee table, and turned the TV on. Then he checked the box's contents. Besides donuts and loaves of bread, there were several three-layer cream-filled cakes, and he got a knife from the kitchen to cut a massive slice.

"Cake is a sometimes food!" squeaked a voice.

Jarrett scowled at Elmo, who was shaking his finger on TV and basically acting retarded. ...Why did adults think little kids wanted mentally-challenged mentors? Jarrett flipped Elmo the finger. "*Any* food is a sometimes food when you don't got money to buy it, dumb-ass!"

Elmo warned him about getting obese as he stuffed down the cake in huge hungry bites. Then he took the box into the kitchen and put Panther-boy on the fridge with a magnet like his mother had done with his little-kid art. He found a can of sardines in a cupboard and made a couple of sandwiches. Then he put most of the things in the fridge and ate his meal with a glass of water while Elmo advised him to eat vegetables and go out and play for an hour every day.

"Which could get your ass capped around here," said Jarrett. "I rather be 'obese' than dead, you privileged little dork."

Finally, he took a look at the kitchen: dirty dishes filled the sink, the floor was screaming to be swept, and the garbage can smelled like something dead. He snagged the broom, kicked off his shoes, and did what had to be done.

After cleaning the kitchen, he swept out and straightened the living room. He flipped the cushions on the couch like his mother used to do every week, and found three dollars and fifteen cents. Then he cut a square from the bakery box, found a roll of cellophane tape, and went to patch the broken window.

It was early evening and growing dark. The breeze sighed in with an eerie whisper, seeming to chill the air in his room. He saw the ancient hearse roll up and stop in the funeral home's driveway. He'd been distracted watching for cops so he hadn't even looked at the place when coming home from the bakery; but the boy had been at work again planting flowers around the yard. Jarrett paused before taping the patch, watching the tall slim shape emerge like a shadow into the dying day. The boy was wearing his long leather coat, but shed it now to reveal he was shirtless... nearly naked actually, his jeans so low on his slender hips he would have gotten busted uptown. He opened the hearse's big back door, and Jarrett saw it was full of more flowers... and something else.

A coffin!

It was shaped like an old-time movie coffin, made of beautiful ebony wood with gleaming brass handles and bright polished fittings... though it looked disturbingly small. Jarrett recalled his homey's coffin, also smaller than a man's; but that had been a pauper's casket, hardly more than a cardboard box.

For all his willowy slenderness, the midnight boy seemed surprisingly strong, hefting the coffin onto a shoulder and bearing it into the house. He almost lost his jeans on the way, but that wasn't funny because of his burden. A shiver ran through Jarrett's body: he remembered something he'd read in a book, about someone walking over your grave.

The boy disappeared with the small black coffin, and Jarrett finished patching the window. Then he studied the broken door: the landlord would have to fix it, but he'd want extra money besides the rent.

And the rent was due in a week.

Thinking about money made Jarrett angry... what was the stupid stuff anyway that made people want it so bad they would kill? Just pieces of paper with dead men on them! He wished he lived in Panther-boy's jungle where no one would need any money.

The apartment seemed big and empty now as he wandered through its darkening rooms. He peeped from a window to check for the cop. The rat-colored car wasn't there anymore, but he still had a feeling of being watched. He really felt like a panther-boy, but trapped in a world that hated his kind. Back in the graveyard playing with Robby he'd felt so strong and sure of himself, but now that feeling had died with the sun.

Jarrett returned to the kitchen and looked at his Panther-boy cartoon, which lifted his spirit a little. He taped it onto his dresser mirror, hoping it would cheer up his room, then drifted into his mother's room. The man had made a mess of it, just like he'd fucked up everything else. Jarrett's fists clenched as he gazed around... if only he'd been stronger! If only he'd been a real Panther-boy! A secret mutant animorph hero! But that was a childish thing to think. He had no powers but those of his mind.

On the chest of drawers was a photograph, taken at K-Mart two years before of Jarrett and his mom. She had looked happy, though working two jobs. He remembered her coming home at midnight, then getting up at six o'clock to do it all over again. Robby was right; she'd done it for him.

So, what could he do for her?

He saw himself in the mirror, and shifted his eyes to the picture again. He'd also looked happy two years ago, a cushion of baby-chub padding his cheeks and hiding the outlines of muscles to come; but now he looked like Robby had said... lean and mean, ferocious and fierce. His eyes, once wide in innocence, were narrow and wary now, and his lips didn't rest in a smile anymore. People would see him the way he was now and never believe he'd played with toys, laughed at stories of Winnie The Pooh, and believed in Elmo's silly-ass shit.

Or hugged Robby in sweet-smelling grass.

That was still his real inside, but how long would it be until he forgot and his inside became like his outside?

Again he felt watched and went to the window. A rat-colored car sat across the street. How long would it be until Panther-boy was captured and locked in a cage?

He snagged what was left of the bakery box and stuffed the man's possessions inside. There was nothing worth trying to pawn; the clothes were cheap and pimpish, and all the jewelry fake. Jarrett opened a window and flung the box into an alley Dumpster. "I hope you burnin' in hell!" he muttered. "An' it hurts a lot!"

He took a shower and put on his clothes, ignoring the cold still haunting his room despite the patch on the window. Then he dusted off the model airplane that sat atop his chest of drawers. There were storybooks, too, lined up by the mirror. He selected one of his favorites, gave Panther-boy a wistful glance, then picked up Robby's skateboard and headed off to see his mom.

The rat-colored car was still at the curb, but there was no one inside. Maybe the cop was checking the Dumpster to see what Jarrett had thrown away? Let him paw through poor-people's trash to see what Jarrett could live without!

Jarrett rolled past the old funeral home. The hearse's back door was still yawning wide, its satin interior brimming with flowers. Jarrett tailed to a wary stop. He studied the house, its front door shut, its windows dark, the drapes all drawn as if in mourning. Should he ask a question? But, the boy was probably busy, maybe preparing the little coffin. ...Or maybe dressing a small kid-corpse. Jarrett snatched a handful of roses. His mother needed their sweet smell of life a lot more than a dead person did.

THIRTEEN

The rehab center looked peaceful as Jarrett came in from the night. Lamps on tables glowed here and there, giving the place a homey look, and people sat reading or watching TV. Most, Jarrett noted, were women, as if men were afraid to ask for help. Or maybe admit they needed help. A few of the – guests? -- were only girls not much older than Jarrett. They peeped him out as he crossed the room with his battered skateboard and boosted roses.

He hadn't expected his mom to be down in the lobby tonight; this was her first long day of withdrawal, and he thought of a sound-proof cell. But, Mrs. Davis's smile was warm as Jarrett reached the top of the stairs and saw her sitting at a desk.

"That limp of yours is just about gone. Skateboardin' must be good therapy."

Jarrett recalled running free through the graveyard, chased by a "lion" while dodging angels. Maybe that was good therapy, too? "Is my mom all right?" he asked.

Mrs. Davis's smile didn't die. "She's doin' a lot better than I expected. I think you was right that it wasn't good stuff... didn't get much of a hold on her." She frowned. "Not as much as that dirty man did, makin' her feel like she wasn't worth nothin'. I took her some orange juice a while ago, an' she managed a few bites of supper."

"Can I see her?"

"That's just what she's needin' the most right now, an' I'll find a vase for those pretty roses."

"Here, you can have one."

"Thank you, Jarrett."

81

A lamp on the bed table cast a soft light, and the room, like the lobby, looked peaceful. His mother was wearing a new bathrobe, and sat in the chair by the window. A little TV was atop the dresser showing the Discovery Channel, but she seemed to be gazing out at the bay, at the lights of ships in the distance. Jarrett also looked into the night, thinking that somewhere between here and there, forgotten, aban-doned, lay Robby's graveyard.

He saw his mom was trembling, and her smile seemed strained when she turned to him. Jarrett quickly took her hand. They hugged, she drawing him tightly against her. He wished he was chubby and soft like Robby instead of so hard and unforgiving. He didn't know what to say so he asked, "How was dinner?"

"Real good." His mom also seemed to be searching for words. "Nice young girl brought it up to me."

"Musta been Martin," said Jarrett. "She done this bandage on my arm."

New pain appeared on his mother's face... pain for him, he realized.

"Looks like you got it all dirty," she said. "I should be watchin' over you."

Jarrett pressed his mother's hand. "You will, mom. Soon." He smiled and added, "You just need to rest awhile... like get back your strength to fight all the shi... bad stuff."

This seemed to ease her mind a bit. "What you been doin' today, son? An' where you get these pretty roses?"

Playing in a graveyard and boosting roses out of a hearse didn't sound like cheerful things. "I... found someplace where flowers were growin'. An' I been hangin' with my new friend. The one I told you about. An' I cleaned up the house today. I'ma cover the rent money, too."

"Not by... doin' what you were doin'?"

"I'm never gonna do that again." Jarrett pulled out his key. "Gonna figure out how to use this."

His mother looked puzzled. "That's just the key to your room, son."

"Yeah, I know," said Jarrett. "But, it sorta... symbolic. Like I was sayin' yesterday, we all got keys if you think about it. We just gotta figure out what they can open."

His mother smiled again. "Sounds like one of those fairytale stories I used to read to you at night."

"Guess it is in a way." Jarrett showed her the old storybook. "I brung this along, *The Wind In The Willows*. I know it kinda silly. But, it happy-silly, kinda. Maybe you like me to read you some? You could sit there an' look at the lights... unless you wanna watch TV?"

"It's a show about Easter Island, but I wasn't really watchin' it. Hearin' your voice sound better to me than lookin' at ol' stone faces."

Jarrett read for about half an hour until Mrs. Davis came quietly in with a vase and a small paper cup with two pills and advised Jarrett's mother should rest. He said goodbye with the three magic words and kissed his mom goodnight, adding he'd be back tomorrow and not to worry about anything. Then he asked, "Can I take one of your roses to Martin?"

"That's real nice of you, son."

Mrs. Davis checked Jarrett's bandage as they walked down the hall to the staircase. "Where you pick up that mud? An' those grass stains on your jeans? Y'all go to a park?"

"It's... like a park," said Jarrett.

"Y'all let Martin look at your arm. After all, she need the practice."

Most of the kitchen lights were off. The dishes were washed and stacked on shelves, while pots and pans were hung from their hooks. Jarrett smelled beans and rice as he entered, which made his stomach growl. Martin was perched on a stool at a table reading her school science book. Her pose made Jarrett think of Robby sitting on his tombstone. A laptop was open in front of her, and Martin tapped keys, making notes. An ancient little radio, like a prehistoric ghetto-blaster, was tinnily tuned to the old-school station and playing a silly Nucleus song. Martin was clad in the same faded jeans, but now she was wearing a wife-beater that clung to her contours enticingly tight. She sat half-facing away from the door, intent on her book beneath a light bulb.

Jarrett paused to peep her out... her honey-bronze skin, her natural hair, and the lush round curves of her body. He thought she looked very huggable. "Um, yo, Martin."

Martin looked up, and her chubby cheeks dimpled. "Hi, Jarrett."

Jarrett came over. "Miz Davis said you might wanna check out my arm." He glanced at the little radio: its sound was almost skeletal. Had people actually listened to those and thought they were hearing music? "An' I brung you this... like, a rose by its real name."

"Thank you, it's pretty an' smells real nice." Martin took the rose, then studied Jarrett and smiled again. "You're the first person I ever met who dresses worse than me."

"Thought we been there already?" said Jarrett. "There's more important things in life than frontin' dumb-ass ghetto glam."

"Boy wins another cigar," said Martin. "You hungry? Got red beans an' rice leftover tonight. A big bowl of pudding, too. I can check out your arm when I finish my homework."

Jarrett's stomach growled again... the sandwiches hadn't been much for lunch. "Sure."

Martin put the rose in a water glass, then piled a plateful of food for Jarrett. She got him a bowl of vanilla pudding and poured him a tall glass of milk. Then she returned to her homework. Jarrett ate across the table, perched on another stool. The food was delicious, including the pudding, but his eyes kept drifting back to Martin, shifting often from her face -- thoughtful as she studied the book -- to her figure beneath the tight-clinging shirt. Martin seemed intent on her work -- like getting an A on a science test was something really important -- yet Jarrett felt he should say something.

"Um... cool laptop."

Martin laughed. "My dad found it at the dump."

"People thowin' *computers* away?"

"It's five years old. That's like an antique in computer time."

"Just 'cause somethin's old don't mean it ain't good no more."

"You don't have a computer?" asked Martin.

"Couldn't afford one. Even before all the shit happen."

"I'll ask dad to look for another one, usually he just runs 'em over. ...If you don't mind a dump computer?"

"Ain't scared of a little garbage." Then Jarrett added, "That's a real pretty bracelet. You make it yourself?"

"Thank you," said Martin. "Made it last year. I like leather. It smells sort of wild an' untamed."

"Yeah," agreed Jarrett. "It does smell untamed."

Martin smiled. "Like you."

"...I sweat a lot."

"I didn't mean that in a bad way."

"Oh," said Jarrett. "Um, this is really good food. Your mom do the cookin'?"

"I made the pudding."

"It rocks."

"Thanks."

"Um, that the same book I got in school. ...I remember seein' you there."

Martin looked up again. "I take that as a compliment. Nobody notices people like me."

"I did."

"I saw you in the hall a few times. An' out by the gates. You always seemed preoccupied."

Jarrett shrugged. "Had me a lot to be occupied with."

"I heard you were a dealer."

"Not a very good one."

"I think that's a contradiction in terms. 'Specially when you're wearin' dreads."

Jarrett shrugged again. "I never got into real Rasta stuff, like peace an' love an' one world, it was just cheaper to let my hair grow." He fingered his locks and sighed. "I wasn't a very good Rasta. ...Wasn't a very good anything, I guess."

"Why do you think that?" asked Martin.

Jarrett explained what had happened, how the man had messed up his life and his mom's. "An' how could I go to the cops?" he finished, "When he got my mom addicted to shit so she woulda got busted, too?"

"You couldn't have," said Martin. "Sometimes the law is like a bulldozer; once it gets started it's hard to stop."

85

"Yeah," agreed Jarrett. "An' it run over anything gets in its way. But, I guess the cops know I was slangin'."

Martin shrugged. "You an' fifty other kids. ...A cop came in here just before supper. Detective, I guess, in regular clothes. He talked to Mrs. Davis."

Jarrett felt angry, as if the cop had invaded his space... and his mother's peace. "A white guy with short blond hair?"

"Yeah."

"That's Locke," said Jarrett. "He watchin' me. Probably thinks I'm wicked."

"Don't worry about what he thinks," said Martin. "God knows you're good."

Again Jarrett shrugged. "God might judge me when I'm dead, but the cops are judgin' me now. ...So, you believe in God?"

"Sometimes," said Martin. "When I see people get better here. That's the kind of God I believe in. A God who helps people. Who rolls up his sleeves an' gets dirty. Kinda like my dad." She smiled. "You make me believe in Him, too."

"Why?" asked Jarrett.

"Same reason, you're helpin' your mom."

Jarrett glanced down at his jeans. "An' I dirty?"

"It's good dirt. Honest dirt. Maybe it bothers some people, but I don't think it bothers God." Martin closed the book and shut down the computer. "Let's have a look at your dirty ol' arm."

They walked to the little medical room, and Martin unlocked its door with a key from her pocket switched on the overhead light. "Up on the table again."

"Want me to take off my shirt?" asked Jarrett.

"'Course," said Martin professionally. "Gotta check those ribs."

"Oh, sure." Jarrett hopped onto the black leather table and stripped off his ragged old shirt.

Martin seemed all business now. "What you been doin' today? Rollin' around on a muddy lawn?"

Jarrett felt warmth when Martin touched him, gently squeezing his sides. "Um... sorta. ...Nice day."

Martin smiled. "Get a tan?"

86

Jarrett laughed and spread his arms. "Can't you tell?"

"Where did you go? A park?"

"...It's... like a park," said Jarrett. "But, not like ours around here. More like the parks they got uptown. But, prettier, an' private, an' a lot more peaceful."

"Sounds like a secret place," said Martin, starting to unwrap the bandage. "Maybe even magic."

"Could be a secret I guess," said Jarrett. "But I ain't sure about magic. ...Um, you ever go to parks?"

"It isn't much fun goin' places alone."

"Yeah," agreed Jarrett. "There's lots of things that ain't much fun when you gotta do 'em alone. ...But, um, you feel good about yourself, don't you?"

Martin gave him a curious look. "Most of the time. I ain't much but I'm all I got."

"I ain't much, neither," said Jarrett.

Martin raised an eyebrow. "Ever look in a mirror?"

"Huh?"

Martin smiled again. "You're kind of hard to believe in. Like magic."

Jarrett looked down at himself. "This only my outsides. I don't wanna be liked just 'cause of that."

Martin laughed. "I wouldn't like you just 'cause of that."

"What if I was chubby?" asked Jarrett. "Or way fat?" He laughed and patted his pecs. "Like, with boy-breasts?"

"Then there'd be more outsides to like, but it's the inside that matters. That's where the magic lives." Martin inspected the wound again. "You should have let me stitch this."

"Can you really do that?"

"'Course, but it's too late now. ...Seems to be healin' pretty fast, but you gonna have a nasty scar."

Jarrett shrugged. "I live with it."

"Everybody will think you're bad."

"That's outsides, too. ...Anyway, you know how it happen, I done it myself. How bad is that?"

"You could lie."

"I don't like to lie. I only lie when I gotta."

"Did you lie to the cop?"

"A little," said Jarrett. "But I think he knew when I was. He gots a son about my age... 'less he was lyin' to me about that. Cops can lie about anything if they say they tryin' to find the truth."

"He could have put you in jail," said Martin.

"He said I couldn't leave town."

"Were you plannin' to?"

"Yeah, right."

"He could have shot you and said you scared him."

Jarrett scowled. "I supposed to be grateful for that?"

"Thank God for small favors," said Martin. "So, how's the ankle tonight? Want some more horse liniment?"

"No thanks." Then Jarrett asked, "Um... you ever got time to go somewhere? I know a place, an' it's peaceful an' private."

"Like where you got my bandage all dirty?"

"Yeah. ...Um, I don't got money for movies an' cool stuff."

"You're really hard to believe in," said Martin.

"Maybe it's my tail."

"Excuse me?"

"I tell you about it some day."

Martin smiled. "I could always find the time to go somewhere peaceful an' private with you."

FOURTEEN

The moon was rising ghostly-white, climbing above the Oakland hills like the glowing dome of a gigantic skull when Jarrett arrived at the graveyard gates. He'd skated home after leaving the center to get some things for Robby, and thought he'd seen the rat-colored car furtively following him through the streets, so he'd left the house through the basement door, cut through several alleys, and seemed to have lost Detective Locke.

The moon cast shadows of stone-robed angels, and Robby sat in his usual place atop the mossy tombstone. He was reading his book in the street lamp's glow, and looked like the chubby water-boy who someone had dressed in ragged clothes and worn-out sneaks for a Halloween joke.

Jarrett unlocked the gates. "Guess Eric didn't show today," he said as Robby hopped down from the stone and stashed his book in the grass.

"He always come at night," said Robby.

"How long it been since you seen him?" asked Jarrett, re-locking the rusty chain.

"Can't remember, but I forget stuff. ...I warned you 'bout that, didn't I?"

"Yeah," said Jarrett, pocketing his key. "If I didn't know you better, I think you was doin' drugs."

"Just high on life." Robby spread his arms. "Which is easy to be where everyone's dead." He noticed the paper bag Jarrett carried. "What'cha got there?"

"Wait an' see," said Jarrett. "You seem to be good at waitin'."

89

They walked through the dew-sparkled grass to the crypt. Jarrett squeezed in through the doorway and pulled a candle out of the bag.

"How it go out there with the livin'?" asked Robby, appearing out of the darkness as Jarrett lit the candle.

Jarrett stuck the candle in the forty-ounce bottle. "Better than I expected. I might even start to like livin' again."

Robby smiled. "You see Martin today?"

"A little while ago. ...Surprised you remembered her name."

"So am I," said Robby. "Maybe it's havin' you to talk to. Like, resurrectin' my brain."

The crypt was still warm from the sun-heated stone, and Jarrett shed his coat. "You dig up somethin' to eat today?"

"I usually go for McMaggots, but Colonel Corpse was havin' a special on chicken in a casket."

Jarrett opened the bag. "Here's a deuce of cream-filled cakes."

"Woah!" said Robby. "Food like that make life worth livin'!"

"No matter what Elmo says." Jarrett gave Robby one of the cakes and reached back into the bag. "Found some coin in the couch today. Coulda scored us a forty, but I figured milk go better with cake... *real* milk, not that milk-flavored water shit they give you at school." He pulled out a half-gallon jug.

"Moo work, too," said Robby, cracking the seal of the plastic cake box as if he was baring a treasure.

"Damn!" said Jarrett. "Forgot to bring forks."

"No prob," said Robby. "Let's get messy! You might wanna take off your shirt. ...Or is it too cold?"

"It still plenty warm in here." Jarrett shed his shirt, and Robby did the same.

"Now, you does it like this," said Robby, plopping down on the floor. He scooped up a handful of creamy cake and stuffed it into his mouth.

Jarrett laughed. "I down with it."

It was cool to be eating like this, thought Jarrett, doing everything Elmo said not to, like a sweet and silly sin. They finished the cake and he sighed, patting his belly which bulged a bit. "Feel like I'm balanced on somethin'. Like, between good an' bad

90

somehow."

"Don't lose your balance," said Robby. "We still got another cake."

The boys stuffed down the second cake and guzzled the last of the milk. Jarrett unbuttoned his jeans halfway and sprawled against a slab. "Always heard that havin' sex was supposed to be the coolest feelin', but now I ain't so sure."

Robby lay in a similar pose, his back to the nameless slab. "Ever have sex?"

"Nah. Unless this counts," said Jarrett, making the obvious hand gesture. "But I think about it a lot. Don't you?"

"Used to," said Robby. "But it don't seem important no more."

Jarrett frowned. "I think you been in this boneyard too long."

Robby laughed. "I can still get a bone of my own."

Jarrett shook his head. "Sometimes you gotta get serious, man. Like what you told me yesterday... sometimes it hurts to be a kid, an' maybe sometimes it has to hurt, an' if you can't learn to deal with it now, how you gonna deal with it later?"

"Did I say that? It sound pretty smart."

"Way too smart to waste on dead people."

Robby looked thoughtful. "There's worse places I could be."

Jarrett thought of Detective Locke, who could lock him up in a lot worse place. And he'd probably made him more suspicious by losing him tonight. *If you're not guilty, then why are you hiding?*

But, what was he supposed to do, live his life as if on parole for the crime of being black and alive? Be afraid to commit the smallest sins, even the sweet and silly sins? The kind of sins kids *should* commit despite what Elmo said.

FIFTEEN

Jarrett lay on his back on the slab of a tomb, gazing up at the rose-tinted sky as dawn slowly came to the graveyard. He was barefoot and shirtless in only his jeans after washing off the crumbs of cake and smears of frosting in the pond. His hands were folded on his chest, and a flower was clasped between his fingers.

"You doin' the King Tut again," said Robby, wading his way through waist-high grass that sparkled with silvery dew. Like Jarrett he wore only jeans, the brassy moons of his bottom half bare, belly bouncing and boy-breasts bobbing. He lay down on the tomb beside Jarrett and crossed his arms under his head. "But you look like you dreamin' instead of dirt-nappin'."

"King Tut had a lot to dream about."

"Yeah," agreed Robby. "Had him a whole big country to run. An' pyramids to build."

Jarrett tossed the flower away. "All I gotta do is pay the rent, but that seem harder than pyramid buildin'." He turned his face to Robby's, their noses just inches apart. "Funny," he said. "When I'm here I feel different."

"Different?" asked Robby.

"It hard to explain. ...But, I feel like if someone come up to them gates they couldn't see neither one of us now."

Robby smiled. "You can't be a ghost 'cause you didn't die... unless I'm only imagining you. Like, I dreamed you up because I was lonely an' you're my imaginary friend."

"I could say the same about you," said Jarrett. "But that ain't what I mean." He glanced toward the gates and the city beyond. "When

92

I'm in here, then nothin' out there seem to matter no more. Like, my life was just a dream an' I only wake up in here."

"Then why you worryin' about the rent?"

"Can't you be serious, Robby? ...Sometimes, anyway."

"Aight, this is me bein' serious." Robby lay a bronze hand on Jarrett's black chest. "I feel a heart an' it's beatin' in there. An' where there's life there's always hope. Even if it hurt sometimes." He thought for a moment. "An' maybe dreams are a way to rest... like to get back your strength to keep on hopin' so you can make your dreams come true."

Jarrett clasped Robby's hand. For thirteen years he'd lived in a city surrounded by thousands of people, yet he'd never felt as close to someone as this boy who cribbed in a graveyard. It was almost as if he had *been* a ghost, crying unheard in the darkness and cold, longing for warmth and light... and hope. And only Robby had heard him. He pressed Robby's hand, feeling its warmth. "Sometimes you scare me."

"Why?" asked Robby.

Jarrett looked up at the lightening sky. "'Cause when you like somebody... an' you love somebody... you also worry about 'em. Like, if they got enough to eat. Are they all right... an' are they happy." He met Robby's eyes. "I never been close to nobody before. Not this close, like you an' me. Close enough to hug like we done. An' even closer than that." Jarrett felt shy. "Like, here we are, two dudes holdin' hands."

"That's cool 'cause nobody can see us."

"I thought you was bein' serious?"

Robby squeezed Jarrett's hand. "I am. But, you're close with your mom."

Jarrett shrugged. "That's a different kind of close. Like, the close every kid should get, even if some of 'em don't. ...The kinda close that makes you strong so you can deal with things that hurt."

Robby laced his fingers with Jarrett's. "Life is gonna be scary sometimes, just like it's gonna hurt sometimes. The world don't work accordin' to Elmo."

Jarrett sighed. "Guess I sound like a little kid, huh?"

93

"You sound like a man to me," said Robby. "I never knew very many. My dad was a man till he lost his key, or maybe forgot he had one. Then he turned into a little kid, an' everything that went wrong in his life was somebody else's fault. That's how little kids think. But, I think I know what a man sounds like, an' I think I'm hearin' one now." He reached behind Jarrett's ear, and there was the key like a magic trick. He lay it on Jarrett's chest. "Don't lose this, man."

Jarrett gazed out beyond the walls. The city was quiet on Sunday morning and he could hardly hear its sounds.

Robby followed Jarrett's eyes. "You got a lot of livin' to do. An' dreamin' an' hopin'... an' probably hurtin'... before you check into a place like this."

Jarrett patted the marble slab. "You think this is forever? I know they only bones down there, but what about the person they was?" He sat up and brushed the moss away to read the name in stone. "Randolph Carter: 1890 to 1937. You figure he down there with his bones? Or did he get to go somewhere else? The *real* him that lived in his bones. The inside part, like maybe his soul?"

Robby looked at the rising sun. "You talkin' 'bout heaven? Streets made of gold like a preacher say? People wearin' white nightgowns an' flappin' their wings in the clouds?"

"I used to think heaven was like that," said Jarrett. "When I was a little kid an' mom still took me to church. But, a heaven like that would be boring as hell."

"Maybe they got asses to ride?"

"Dammit, this is serious, man. There's gotta be somethin' better than that."

"Better than just doin' nothin' forever?"

Jarrett frowned. "I don't wanna do nothin' forever. If I spend my life tryin' to be good, an' tryin' to make my dreams come true, then why would I wanna do nothin' forever? That don't make no sense to me. An' neither does goin' to hell if I'm bad."

"What don't make sense about hell?" asked Robby.

"Burnin' forever just 'cause you was bad for a few dumb-ass years when you was alive. What's a few years compared to *forever?*" Jarrett thought for a moment. "Gettin' punished forever is too much too late. Like sendin' a kid to prison for life 'cause he boosted a loaf of bread. You punish somebody to show 'em they bad. Like, makin' a little kid stand in a corner. To teach 'em they bad so they learn to be good. But, why punish someone forever? You'd never know if it worked. That mean you didn't *care* if it worked."

"What about the man?" asked Robby. "He messed up your life an' hurt your mom. Don't you want him punished forever?"

Jarrett thought about that, feeling the sun as it warmed his body, smelling the flowers, hearing birdsong. "If you'd axed me that two days ago, I'd said he *should* be in hell forever. But, now I ain't so sure."

Robby raised an eyebrow. "You sayin' you forgive him?"

Jarrett shrugged. "I don't know. But, if God don't care if His punishment works... if God won't forgive, why should I?" He flexed his bandaged arm, prodded his ribs and wiggled his ankle. The pain was almost gone, and it seemed stupid to call it back, to try to make himself hurt... or to hate what had hurt him. "If there is a hell on the real, there gotta be a way out of it. ...Or maybe some kind of parole at least to see if you learned to be good. If there ain't, then God don't give a shit, an' I can't believe in a god like that."

"But He gave you a chance to be good," said Robby. "By givin' you a life to live."

Jarrett put the key in his pocket, then swung his feet to the ground. "Check this out."

He led the way to a weathered headstone on a small grassy grave by the pond... the grave where they'd hugged yesterday. A very young angel watched over it, sitting on a pedestal. Jarrett pointed to words at its feet. "Christopher... somethin'... can't read the rest of his name. 1899 to 1912. He was only thirteen when he died." Jarrett studied the sad stone boy... long curly locks, chubby and cute, and clad in what looked like an uncertain diaper. Maybe it represented the boy whose bones lay buried below?

"How much of a chance did he get?" said Jarrett. "To learn what life was all about an' make a choice between bad an' good? To check out what his key could open. You sayin' God judged him on thirteen years then took him to heaven or sent him to hell? An' what would be worse for somebody his age... bein' punished by burnin' forever in hell, or bein' bored by doin' nothin' till all the stars go out?"

Robby said, "I read all the names in here already." He patted the angel-boy's stony locks. "Chris ain't the youngest, there's babies, too. One didn't live a whole day."

Jarrett looked at the rising sun now clearing the eastern hills. "They gotta get another chance, or God don't give a shit."

Robby sat down on Christopher's grave, leaning back against the stone and crossing his arms behind his head. "Maybe hell is somethin' else?"

"Like what?" asked Jarrett.

Robby pointed down. "What if, instead burnin' forever, your punishment was to lay down there an' rot with your skeleton bones?"

Jarrett shrugged. "If you dead, so what? It like sleep without dreams an' you never wake up."

"But, what if you was awake?" asked Robby. "Not alive, just awake."

A chill ran down Jarrett's spine. "What you sayin'?"

"What if you was down there right now, all alone in the dark... but you could hear us talkin' up here?"

Jarrett stared down at the small grassy grave, and another shiver ran through his body. But after a moment he said, "I already been in that kinda hell... layin' all alone in the dark an' thinkin' about my fucked-up life over an' over again."

"But it wasn't you who fucked it up."

Jarrett sighed. "I know that now. But I didn't know then. I thought it was all my fault somehow... maybe for not bein' good. Or maybe for not bein' strong. Like, God already judged me an' He didn't give a shit what happen to me anymore."

Jarrett sat down beside Robby. "My homey got him a stone. A little one anyway. 'Bout the size of a brick. But, I don't think he under it now." Jarrett looked up at the sky. "Not if there really a God who cares. But, I can't believe he doin' nothin' but floatin' around an' playin' a harp. An' if God sent him to hell, it mean He didn't know him... just like that cop don't know me."

Robby asked, "Think he got another chance?"

"Don't know what to think," said Jarrett. He took a handful of grave dirt and let it fall through his fingers. "Maybe he's... just dead. Game over. Lights out. No hope, no dreams, no key. Maybe that would of happened to me if I'd died that night when you let me come in. All you'd have was a rottin' corpse stinkin' up your crib... 'less you put me in that empty place, behind that slab without no name."

Robby hesitated then said, "I didn't wanna tell you before... in case you couldn't handle it... but there's already somebody in there."

Jarrett's mouth fell open. He sprang up and stared at the little stone house. "W-who?"

"Does it matter?" said Robby. "He was a kid who hung with the gang... the gang that wasn't. Some other kids capped him." He slapped a hand to his chest, then kicked out his legs and went limp. "Game over, lights out."

"That ain't funny!" snapped Jarrett.

Robby opened his eyes. "Sure wasn't for him."

Jarrett turned toward Robby's crypt. "So... you an' your posse put him in there? ...You told me they opened that slab one time, but you didn't say why."

"I forgot," said Robby. "I did...?"

"Yeah, you did."

Robby shrugged. "It was better than bein' buried like trash by people who didn't know him."

"...Well... yeah," said Jarrett. "But it *creepy*, man! I been sleepin' next to a dead kid!"

Robby laughed. "There's eleven other dead people in there. Skeletons anyway. What difference another one make?"

"But, that slab ain't cemented shut like the others. Wouldn't there be... a smell?"

Robby pulled up a flower and smelled it. "Probably was at first. But, he wasn't a mummy like little King Tut. ...If you see what I sayin'?"

Jarrett tried to put the grisly picture in time-lapse photography out of his mind. "Guess, after a while... with bugs an' worms an' maggots an' stuff... there wouldn't be nothin' but skeleton bones."

Robby rolled his eyes. "Ya think."

Jarrett looked back at the crypt. "Guess I could handle bones. ...I mean bones would be better than somethin' that wasn't. Or not all the way."

Robby smiled. "I'm sure they all the way by now."

"Did you know him?" asked Jarrett.

"For a little while." Robby yawned and stretched. "But you still got your skin on, doggie-bro. An' you better get busy to stay that way."

SIXTEEN

Jarrett locked the graveyard gates and watched as Robby went to the tombstone and climbed on top with his book. Jarrett waved goodbye, then decked Robby's board and skated away. Keeping his skin on didn't seem easy no matter how busy he wanted to get. He thought of the few legitimate jobs the law would let him do. A paper route? He needed a bike. Sell cookies or candy for a church? He'd have better luck if he looked like Robby instead of a dangerous Panther-boy.

But, even if he could do those things, he couldn't make two-hundred dollars by the end of the coming week. It wasn't fair that he wanted to work and the law made working a crime for him, but that was Elmo's kind of law in Elmo's kind of TV heaven where kids were never hungry or hurt and were only supposed to play all day while eating healthy food. He fingered the skeleton key in his pocket: to open a door you had to find one.

Suddenly, a snarling shape came charging out of nowhere! Jarrett tumbled off the board, shredding skin from his elbows and knees, as the junkyard dog slammed into the fence. The animal seemed insane, a mindless, raging, hateful thing. Jarrett leaped up and almost ran. Then anger flared inside him, a red kind of rage at everything wrong... he was days away from being homeless, and maybe closer to being caged, and even this dog wouldn't leave him in peace!

A broomstick lay in the gutter trash, and he snatched it up like a spear. His own teeth flashed as he charged to the fence and jabbed at the dog through the mesh. The animal yelped and retreated a little, still baring its fangs and snarling. Then, footsteps clattered through canyons of junk, and Jarrett saw the two older boys in their greasy old jeans and battered boots. They looked even more like twins today as they chased the dog off with curses then came to the fence with identical grins.

"Yo, little man," said the blond boy. "You look like a hunter with that spear."

"Yeah," agreed the black dude. "But, if you tryin' to hunt up a meal, I don't think Satan gonna taste good."

"His name is Satan?" asked Jarrett.

The black dude laughed. "That's what the boss calls him."

Jarrett tossed the broomstick away. "Don't care what the hell his name is, he got no right scarin' people."

The blond boy said, "He can only scare you if you let him."

"Yeah," agreed the black. "He's the one locked up, not you."

Jarrett's anger faded. "...Yeah, guess he is. ...In his own hell of junk. ...You guys work on Sunday?"

The black boy laughed. "No rest for the wicked this side of the grave."

The white one added, "But, Sundays we work for our own wicked selves."

Jarrett sighed. "I can't even do that."

The black boy cocked his bushy head. "Wuttup, man?"

"Yeah," said the white, shaking back his tangled mop. "I seen faces that long on Easter Island."

Jarrett remembered the TV show his mom had been watching at the center. "You been there?" he asked.

"Not yet," said the black dude.

"But, we gonna go soon," said the white.

"On a airplane?" asked Jarrett.

"We buildin' a boat," said the black dude. "We gonna be sailin' wherever we want."

"Anywhere in the world," said the blond.

Jarrett could see only junk all around, like a rusty graveyard for dead machines. "You buildin' a boat in *there*?" he asked.

"Sure," said the white dude. "We got everything we need."

"She's a schooner," added the black. "Forty-footer. Wanna see her?"

Jarrett knew nothing at all about boats; and the concept of actually building a boat and sailing anywhere in the world was more than a little amazing. The dudes could have said they were building a starship and Jarrett would have been just as amazed. "Sure. ...But, what about Satan?"

The black boy laughed. "He won't have the fence to protect him from you."

The blond boy unlocked the gate. Then they walked between towering mountains of junk back to the rear of the yard. The dog was nowhere in sight, but Jarrett could feel it watching him, which made him think of the cop. They passed a small tin shack. A faded sign said OFFICE, but the door was padlocked. There was another, larger shed, but with only a roof and three walls. Its floor was dirt, soaked with oil, and sagging wooden benches inside were piled with old electric motors and greasy parts from cars and trucks. Then, Jarrett stopped to stare in wonder. Against the back fence, surrounded by junk, was the graceful shape of a big sailboat. It was made of steel, and the metal was rusty, but that didn't make it any less cool.

The blond boy pointed to a ladder. "Welcome aboard."

The black dude added, "We still got the woodwork to do inside, but you get a idea what she gonna look like."

Jarrett climbed up to the schooner's deck. The entire boat was red with rust, but the workmanship looked strong and sturdy as far as he could tell. Most of the fittings -- the portholes and boat things, the two tall masts -- had been seemingly salvaged from other boats. Jarrett went to a hatch and looked down in the cabin. The interior wasn't finished yet, but he remembered pictures he'd seen and imagined lots of varnished wood. He climbed down inside. The boys were already living aboard. There was a stove and a stainless-steel sink, a table, and sort of a built-in couch. Clothes, books, and personal things were scattered all around. Toward the front of the boat was a little bathroom, and there was a bed in the V of the bow. Jarrett thought that was cool: if one boy couldn't sleep at night he

101

would have the other to talk to.

"Cool!" he said, climbing back to the ground.

"She be in the water by fall," said the black dude.

"We named her *Hope*," said the white. "Gonna sail her around the world."

Jarrett studied the boat again. "Mean you can just go sailin' away an' nobody can stop you?"

The black boy laughed. "Ain't no fence 'round the 'hood, 'cept the one people made in their minds."

Jarrett recalled the detective's warning: *don't leave town*. He felt suddenly lonely here with these boys who had each other and shared a life while dreaming cool dreams of a future. "You dudes got keys," he murmured.

"Say what?" asked the white boy.

"Just thinkin'," sighed Jarrett.

"Don't stop," said the black dude. "Thinkin' gets to be a habit if you do it enough."

"Want a beer?" the blond boy asked, lifting the lid of a rusty ice chest.

"Thanks," said Jarrett, accepting a frosty green bottle. "Never thought you could build somethin' cool out of junk."

The black boy patted the side of the boat. "From rust to rust in sure an' certain hope."

Jarrett remembered the truck driver: *The only stupid questions are the ones you think you're too smart to ask.* ...Or maybe you were scared to ask because you might sound uncool? He drank some beer to brace himself for probably being laughed at. "Any chance of me workin' here? Like, helpin' you dudes with your boat?"

Instead of laughing, the boys exchanged glances. Jarrett went on, though he felt like one of those cookie kids making a sad little speech to sell something. "I gotta pay the rent next week. For me an' my mom. ...She... in rehab now, but she gonna get better soon."

The blond boy nodded. "An' you might get evicted before she comes home?"

"Yeah," said Jarrett.

"Well," said the black. "We pretty much got it down with *Hope*, but the boss always needin' new help. ...You can probably figure why."

"It's hard an' dirty work," said the blond.

"You'll tear up your hands," warned the black. "An' the boss makes Satan look like Elmo."

"Does he treat you guys mean?" asked Jarrett.

The blond boy laughed. "Nah, 'cause we know where the bodies are buried."

The black boy added. "'Least all the cars scrapped without titles. But, you get yourself hurt, he won't know you."

"Nobody know me now," said Jarrett.

"So, when you wanna start?" asked the blond.

"Yesterday," said Jarrett.

"Right on time," said the black boy. He led the way back to the three-sided shed. "This is where we separate metals. All you do is take stuff apart. Kinda like dissectin' corpses." He picked up a car's alter-nator. "The case is aluminum, see? Aluminum goes in that bin over there."

The blond dude added, "The pulley an' screws are steel... go in this bin over here. The rotor inside is mostly copper... goes in that other bin there."

"Here's tools on the bench," said the black boy. "If you ain't sure what metal it is, use this magnet to check it out."

"'Cause aluminum ain't magnetic," said Jarrett.

"You down with it, man," said the blond dude. "The boss will weigh these bins when they full an' pay you by the pound. But, you come an' get one of us when he does or he cheat you out your skin."

The black boy nodded. "You work about ten or twelve hours a day, you can make around thirty dollars."

"An' it be cash," the blond boy added. "'Cause the boss ain't no brother's bookkeeper."

"I can work all day today," said Jarrett. "But, there's three weeks of school before summer vacation. ...Guess I could drop out."

The black boy shook his head. "Nah, man, we ain't havin' that. Maybe school ain't cool, but you gotta learn stuff."

"Yeah," said the blond. "You drop out school, you always be

workin' in places like this."

The black boy asked, "When you get out for the day?"

"Three-thirty," said Jarrett.

"Aight," said the blond. "The boss leaves at five, but you can work as late as you want. You really bust your butt at this job, you can probably make your rent on time an' maybe a little more."

"Lets do this," said Jarrett.

"We'll bring you somethin' for lunch," said the black, and the boys went off to work on their boat. Jarrett wished he had a dream like theirs, and their seemingly certain hope, but his key had actually opened something besides the gates to a graveyard.

The mid-morning sun on the rusty tin roof had turned the shed into an oven, and Jarrett stripped off his shirt. The tools were ancient and worn out: the screwdriver blades were broken or bent, the wrenches were cracked or sprung out of shape, and the massive old vise on one of the benches took every ounce of his strength to turn. But, Jarrett worked hard and was soon pouring sweat, while Satan crept up to watch him. Jarrett's hands grew slick with grease, and his knuckles suffered savagely whenever a wrench or a screwdriver slipped. The head wouldn't stay on the rusty old hammer -- he soon found out when it bonked his knee -- while Satan looked on suspiciously as if Jarrett was going to steal his junk.

The boys brought Jarrett lunch, a tunafish sandwich and a bottle of beer. The heat and alcohol made him sleepy, and he only finished half the brew... after the hammer had bonked him again. He noticed a rusty faucet nearby dripping into a bucket; and Satan snarled at him when he drank. Jarrett found a piece of pipe and kept it close as a weapon. The day was dirty, hot and long, but Jarrett had filled all the bins by sunset. The boys said he'd done a good job; the boss would weigh the stuff in the morning, and they would make sure he didn't cheat.

SEVENTEEN

Jarrett skated wearily home. His hands were cut, his knuckles bloody, and both knees bruised by the treacherous hammer, and yet he felt strong and alive...

Until he saw the rat-colored car under a street lamp across from his house. Detective Locke was reading a paper, but Jarrett knew what was up. He tailed his board and stalked to the car. "What you doin' here?" he demanded.

The man shrugged. "It's a free country, kid."

"For you, anyway."

Locke studied Jarrett a moment, as if noting his many cuts and scrapes, the oil and grease all over his jeans, and probably his sweaty smell. "What have you been doing today?"

"Got me a job in a chop-shop. ...What you probably figure, huh?"

"Don't get smart, kid."

"What my other choice?"

Locke looked thoughtful. "You sound like my son."

"You snoop on him, too?"

"I would if he stayed out all night."

"It a free country, remember?"

"Just doing my job," said Locke.

"'Least you got one."

"Stay with your friend again?"

Jarrett shrugged. "Couldn't sleep so I skated a while."

"Guilty conscience?"

"My conscience be clean as a skeleton bone."

105

"Going to see your mother tonight?"

"Follow me some more an' find out."

The detective frowned. "Be careful, kid. I could notify Child Protective Service about you living alone."

Jarrett scowled back. "If you can't lock me up for murder you gonna get me on Elmo's law?"

Locke looked curious. "Elmo's law?"

"The law you use to protect your son. To tell him to eat right an' play every day. To not talk to strangers, an' brush his teeth, an' never leave the water run. But where was that law when *I* needed help? You never did nothin' till somebody died, an' now you won't leave me in peace!"

"Died, or was murdered, that's still the question."

"He didn't have no right to live when he started killin' my mom an' me!"

"Don't dig yourself a grave, kid."

"...What you sayin'?"

Locke made a note in his book. "I wouldn't say that to a jury."

Jarrett's anger suddenly died. "If you tell the child people, we lose the apartment."

"I know," said Locke, and started the car. "Rest in peace, kid."

Jarrett watched the car's tail lights fade away up the street. Would Locke return to follow him later? There was nothing Jarrett could do about that except watch his back when he went to the graveyard. He had to keep Robby's secret.

He glanced down the street at the old funeral home, dark except for one rear window. Its yard looked pretty with all the new flowers, and the boy had started to paint the front. It would soon be the best-looking house in the 'hood, though its customers probably wouldn't care... at least not the ones who would ride in the hearse. Jarrett remembered the little coffin he'd seen the boy carrying yesterday: did the dude have some business already? Or was it just a sample? Maybe that's why it was small.

Again, Jarrett's room seemed unnaturally cold as breeze whispered in past the cardboard patch. He studied himself in the dresser mirror: it might have been his imagination, but it seemed as if his

106

back was straighter, his chest jutting prouder, his biceps bigger. And the wounded look was gone from his eyes. It was sad to think that the stronger he got the more some people would fear him.

He picked up his model airplane, made motor sounds like a little kid and brought it in for a landing. Supper was bread and "sometimes food" washed down with a glass of water. After his meal he took a shower, then skated off to see his mom. He didn't much care if the cop followed him, though he didn't see the rat-colored car as he rattled though the shadowy streets. At the rehab center, he noticed the girls were peeping him out as he crossed the lobby. That seemed funny: he couldn't have looked very cool, he thought... his jeans were black with grease and oil, and his shirt was no more than a rag. But he held his head high and walked Panther-boy proud.

Mrs. Davis smiled in welcome as Jarrett reached the top of the stairs. She said his mom was doing fine. Jarrett went to his mother's room and read from *The Wind In The Willows*. Then he said the three magic words, and went downstairs to see Martin before going back to the graveyard.

EIGHTEEN

A hand shook Jarrett's shoulder. "Yo! You harder to wake than the dead."

Jarrett opened his eyes to the cheerful smiles of Robby and the dreadlocked skull on the front of Robby's shirt. Webs of shadow still clung in the crypt, and the window was only beginning to glow with the light of a newborn day.

"Time to get vertical, man," said Robby. "You gotta collect your green from the junkyard then get your ass to school."

Jarrett groaned. His body was stiff from yesterday's work, and sleeping on stone hadn't helped. "Thought you forgot stuff."

Robby sat down next to Jarrett. "You too cool to forget."

Jarrett watched as the rising sun brought the window to life in rainbow shades. It would be another peaceful day here in the quiet cemetery; a day of flowers and singing birds, of sun on grass and water-music for skeleton bones with nothing to do. Jarrett wished he could stay here, but finally got to his feet.

"I might not make it back tonight. I gotta work at least till eight if I wanna be sure an' cover the rent. Then I need to see my mom. Then I gotta do my homework. Then... shit!... I gotta do it all over!"

Robby smiled. "A man's gotta to do what a man's gotta do if he wants to make his dreams come true."

Jarrett made a face. "A dead person probably said that."

"Don't make it any less true for the livin'. An' don't trip about me," said Robby. "I'm used to bein' alone."

"Maybe you too damn used to it," said Jarrett before he could stop himself. "An' you don't gotta stay here alone." He took Robby's hand. "Come back with me."

"We been there already," said Robby. "Now, get on your ass an' ride, doggie-bro, or you gonna be late for school."

Jarrett had a silly thought... of dragging Robby home like a prisoner. Robby was strong despite all his chub, though Jarrett knew he was stronger. But, strength didn't give him any right to make anybody do anything.

"Okay," he said reluctantly. He unlocked the door and squeezed past the chain, then paused in the leafy shade of the porch to scan the pretty wildflowers and tall green grass all around. The stony angels still looked sad, but they didn't have any choice.

Robby appeared beside him, and Jarrett took his hand. They walked together through the grass; and the chubby bronze boy was smiling from his little island in the pond. Jarrett unlocked the gates, then turned and gave Robby a hug. "Thanks for all you done for me." He hesitated, then kissed Robby's cheek. "I love you, Robby."

Robby kissed Jarrett's cheek in return. "I love you, too, Jarrett."

NINETEEN

Jarrett worked hard every day at the junkyard from after school until about eight, except for an hour's break around six to go see his mom and have supper with Martin. He skated home through dim-lit streets where the only sounds were his wheels clicking cracks, to finally shower and do his schoolwork. It wasn't surprising he slept like the dead, laying on the living room couch because of the eerie chill in his room, and yet his grades were improving.

Thirty dollars a day was his hope, but he tried to make as much as he could, pushing himself to the edge of his strength, lifting and toting big greasy things, swinging the heavy and treacherous hammer, battling rusty nuts and bolts and often mauling his hands. Pretending to be a panther-boy helped. It was like his inside identity; nobody knew that this raggedy kid was really a mutant jungle cat with hopes and dreams beyond this place.

He hadn't seen the detective in days, though he felt he was still being watched. He knew the cop had been to his school from the way the teachers looked at him -- some sympathetic, a few with fear -- but that was life, he supposed.

He could feel himself getting stronger: his chest muscles strained his tattered shirts, and his biceps bulged like rounded rocks. Despite all the dirt his arm was healing and he'd taken the bandage off. His mother was also regaining her strength, and he knew his own was helping her. And seeing Martin every night gave Jarrett another kind of strength. She was also breaking Elmo's laws -- laws that said one size fit all and every kid should be skeleton skinny and clueless about

110

the real world -- but only made her own life harder by denying her the right to work and the knowledge she needed to survive. She, too, had a key and was trying the locks of all the doors, fences and gates that stood between her and her dreams.

Jarrett missed hanging with Robby, as if there was yet another strength, a kind of soft and gentle strength, that only Robby could give. He planned to see Robby on Friday and spend another night in the crypt.

Thursday it rained. Jarrett shivered at work in the rusty shed while water poured down through its leaky roof and turned the dirt floor into slippery mud, but he'd finally managed to make the rent and hardly noticed the cold. His chest had grown too proud for his coat, which now wouldn't zip all the way, but he felt as if nothing could hurt him. He even astonished Satan by giving him a friendly pat before he left the junkyard.

It was raining hard as he skated home, and he swooshed through puddles and soared over gutters where dark water frothed on its way to the sea. His sodden coat trailed behind like a cape, while his shirt was plastered tight to his chest and his jeans clung heavy and low on his hips. He shot from the alley onto his block and saw the old hearse at the funeral home. Rain rattled down on its night-colored steel, while its chrome glittered bright in a street lamp's glow. PACKARD was spelled on its grinning grille, though Jarrett had never heard that name.

The dark slender boy hadn't rested all week: the ancient house gleamed with a fresh coat of paint and the lawn had been newly reborn. Rosebushes lined the cracked sidewalk and bloomed along the high front porch. A white picket fence had been erected, and climbing vines were checking it out. The dude seemed to rise with the sun every day, clad in nothing but lawless saggers while resurrecting the long-dead home that would also be a home for the dead... or at least a place to say goodbye.

Despite the rain, Jarrett rolled to a stop, pausing to study the tall, narrow house with its steeply-peaked roof and gingerbread trim. It was dark except for one rear window, a somber glow through a deep-purple curtain. Jarrett felt a twinge of guilt... maybe it was stupid, but boosting those roses bothered him. Sure, they'd helped to cheer up his mom, and delighted Martin and Mrs. Davis, but would they have been a better gift if he hadn't stolen them?

Jarrett pictured the slender boy, a near-naked savage when swing-ing his scythe, a little scary when toting a coffin, and yet he seemed gentle somehow. It showed in his delicate face when he smiled, and in his large and long-fingered hands as he smoothed the earth in his new flowerbeds. You'd have to be gentle to deal with the dead... after all, they were helpless.

The one lonely light decided his move. He picked up his board and walked to the house past the white picket fence and the rain-sparkled roses. After climbing the steps to the porch, he gently knock-ed on the door.

To his surprise it swung open a little. He almost expected a ghostly creak, but the boy had probably oiled the hinges. A funeral home shouldn't have spooky doors, but the 'hood was no place to leave one unlocked.

Jarrett got a *déjà vu* feeling, gazing into the gap of darkness and thinking of Robby's house of stone. But there was no chain on this door, and it swung open wide at his touch.

"Um, hello?" he called.

There was only the whispering patter of rain and its trickling splash from the house's eaves. Maybe the boy was asleep? As hard as Jarrett had seen him work, he probably slept like the dead.

"Yo!" called Jarrett. "Your door's unlocked!"

Still no reply. Jarrett stood there unsure what to do while his sodden coat dripped on a new doormat. Heavy drapes shrouded the windows, and he could see almost nothing inside except the shape of a pale chandelier that hung from a vaulted ceiling. But there was probably nothing to see; the house had been empty for decades. The air smelled musty, of dry-rot and dust, sort of a graveyard crypt scent, but so did the air in Jarrett's crib. Of course, the boy had been here a week and might have brought in furniture; but the house *felt* empty, and Jarrett's voice echoed.

Now what, he thought? He regretted his impulse to meet the boy and apologize for boosting the flowers. He noticed the door had an

112

old-fashioned lock and his skeleton key might fit. Should he do the dude a favor?

But, what if he wasn't home right now, and maybe he'd left his key inside and Jarrett locked him out? Yeah, the hearse was here, but you wouldn't go cruising around in a hearse. The boy might have taken a bus somewhere.

"Well, shit," muttered Jarrett. He remembered something he'd read in a book, something a dead person probably said: *No good deed ever goes unpunished*. He hoped it was a joke.

He saw a faint glow across the room. It looked like a light at the end of a hall, maybe the one he'd seen from outside.

"Hello?" he called again.

Jarrett waited another minute, then made a decision and moved toward the light, his steps slow and careful, a hand stretched out, his sneaks making squishy sounds on the floor. This was a damn good way to get capped! ...Or, what if Locke was lurking around and saw him sneak in like a thief? He stopped, glancing back at the open door, and wondered if he should leave while he could.

But then he continued across the room, which seemed to be totally empty. A curtain in shreds concealed a doorway, and the glow leaked out through its ragged holes. Jarrett parted the rotting cloth: beyond was a hall with doors on each side that ran all the way to the back of the house. It seemed like a strange arrangement, until he remembered where he was. Those were probably viewing rooms where people said goodbye to their dead. All the doors were closed except one, down at the end of the hall. The dim light shone from there.

He wondered again if he should leave before the dark boy capped his ass -- or the cop burst in and did -- but he went toward the light anyhow.

"Hello?" he called softly. "Yo, man," he added, "I live next door." ...As if that gave him privileges.

He waited a moment but nobody answered. Reaching the doorway, he peered inside. There was the coffin!

He almost bolted in shock. But, fortunately, the lid was off, revealing only a red silk lining, which looked disturbingly comfortable.

113

The coffin sat on a rough wooden stand, which probably would have been buried in flowers had there been a body to view. Pale white candles flanked it, burning in tall silver holders.

Then, he saw the slender boy asleep in an old velvet chair. He was wearing only his dangerous jeans, and his long-fingered hands lay curled on his belly like peaceful ebony spiders. His legs were stretched out, and his big bare feet were resting atop an old wooden box which bore the word, FORMALDEHYDE. On another such box beside the chair were several massive leather-bound books. There were also Church's Chicken remains, and an empty forty-ounce bottle. Jarrett noted the long leather coat was hung from a hook in a corner, and the scythe leaned against the wall, its big deadly blade looking newly sharpened and glittering in the candle glow.

Jarrett stood, surveying the room. He remembered a picture he'd seen a book of someone "sitting up" with a body... maybe to see if it came back to life. But, the only body in here was the boy's, his slim chest rising with slow, even breaths. The candlelight played on his midnight shape, gently defining his delicate muscles and softly highlighting his fine-boned face. He was beautiful yet masculine and that made Jarrett afraid. He told himself to get out of here.

He crept back up the shadowy hall, wincing each time a floorboard squeaked. Crossing the gloomy living room, he peeped outside to check for the cop. Then he locked the door with his skeleton key.

TWENTY

He ran past the nodding, rain-sparkled roses, then to his house and up the stairs. He slammed and locked the apartment door, then slumped against it panting for breath. A street lamp's glow through the living room window cast rippling shadows across the walls as rain poured off the house's eaves with a rushing watery sound. Garbage cans rattled in the alley below, and the Dumpster made a hollow boom. He recalled the scene in the old death house -- the coffin, the candles, the long spooky hall, and the glimmering Grim Reaper blade -- but the beautiful sleeping boy had frightened him more than anything else.

His heartbeat gradually slowed to normal. He leaned Robby's board against the wall and went to light the iron gas fire that crouched on little clawed feet in a corner. He shed his jacket and peeled off his shirt while his dreadlocks dripped like ice down his back. Then he sat on the floor by the wavering flames to take off his sodden shoes and socks. Finally he wiggled out of his jeans to become Panther-boy at his jungle campfire. Maybe that was childish, even a little Elmo -- though Elmo wouldn't approve of the fire, "not without adult super-vision" -- but it was good to bask in the warmth while shivery tingles ran through his body.

At last warmed up he went to the kitchen, lit the stove and filled a kettle. The clock on the wall, a plastic lion who twitched his tail to the passing of time, was showing a minute past midnight.

Leaving the kettle to boil, he went reluctantly into his room like a little kid into a scary place. He almost had to force himself to pass the broken door. The room felt unnaturally cold, and there was a

115

smell of dampness and dirt. Rain leaked in past the cardboard patch and had puddled across the floor. The rush of water off the roof began to sound like whispering. He had a feeling of being watched and quickly turned on the light. He went to the window and scanned the street but couldn't see anyone.

Then he searched the dresser drawers. Besides the rent, he needed new clothes; his shirts were all ragged, his socks full of holes. He found a pair of faded jeans, their cuffs in ribbons, and ripped at the knees. Like Robby's they were cartoonishly tight and couldn't be buttoned all the way. He scanned himself in the mirror: he really did look like the Panther-boy sketch -- except for the ears and tail -- muscular midnight and savagely scary... at least to people who only saw outsides.

Again he felt watched and spun around, yet nothing was there but his shadow. He returned to the broken window. Raindrops glittered like gold outside in the yellowish glow of the street lamp, and a spiderweb sparkled like amber jewels. A few lights shone in other houses but only made the night seem darker.

"*Déjà vu,*" he murmured. "But, you *have* been here before."

He saw the dim light in the funeral home and again recalled the beautiful boy sleeping alone by the small black coffin. He wondered how many other kids were all alone and lonely tonight. Was Robby sleeping surrounded by bones? Was he warm enough? Had he eaten today? Jarrett wished he'd hugged him more, but that wasn't something dudes often did.

Why not, he wondered? Death was always lurking, and life could be so short. Why be afraid of a hug? Or to say you loved someone.

Breeze whispered in past the leaking patch like clammy fingers over his skin. He seemed to feel eyes on his back and spun around to see nothing again. And again he felt the eerie cold, yet the heater burned bright in the living room only a few feet away. Jarrett shivered violently. He forced himself to walk from the room, though he really wanted to run.

The door buzzer sounded.

Jarrett froze. If that was the cop, it could only mean prison! There was no other reason he'd come after midnight!

116

The buzzer rattled again, and Jarrett tried to think... maybe someone had pushed the wrong button?

He almost jumped when another buzz sounded. For a second he thought of running away. He looked to his room past the splintered door: he could escape out the window...

But, this was his *home*, goddammit! He'd been fighting to keep it with all his new strength! And why should he run like a scared little kid when nothing had actually threatened him?

He tried to make his voice sound hard as he flipped the speaker switch. "Yeah?"

"Jarrett? It's Martin."

"Huh?" said Jarrett stupidly. He looked at the clock in the kitchen: almost 12:30. And the kettle was boiling over! It took a few moments to make his voice work. "Um... hi, Martin. Um, c'mon up."

He punched the unlock button, dashed to the kitchen and turned off the stove, then raced back to open the door. He peered down the dim-lit hallway as a shadow climbed the stairs. A few seconds later Martin appeared, but Jarrett felt a new stab of fear... had something happened to his mom? He searched Martin's face as she came up the hall, but there was a smile on her lips. She wore a black hoodie and beanie cap, and her jeans clung low all soaked with rain. Her school tote was slung on a shoulder and seemed a strange thing to be to packing at midnight.

Jarrett felt more than a little naked in his tightly outgrown and unbuttoned jeans, but at least they were more than a towel. "Um, hi, Martin. Is... somethin' wrong?"

The girl also seemed a little unsure, which wasn't her usual thing. She was holding something in one hand, but Jarrett hardly noticed.

"Hi, Jarrett. Everything's cool. Your mom told me where you lived an' I saw your light walkin' home. I thought you might be up doin' homework."

"Oh," said Jarrett. "Ain't started yet. Um, want some coffee?"

"Sure."

Jarrett stepped back for Martin to enter, and saw what she was holding... a handful of rain-sparkled roses. "Where you get those?"

"They were down on the porch," said Martin. "I thought you

might have dropped 'em."

"...Me?" asked Jarrett. He was sure he hadn't seen any roses when he'd run up the steps. "Why you think they mine?"

"'Cause you brought some like these for your mom."

Had the dark boy left them, Jarrett wondered? And what did it mean if he had? Had he only pretended to be asleep when Jarrett was in the funeral home? Had he been waiting for Jarrett to speak? Maybe for Jarrett to ask a question? He realized a moment had passed and Martin was looking curious. "...Oh. Um, thanks, Martin."

"Better put 'em in water so they'll be fresh for your mom tomorrow."

"...Yeah. Thanks. I give you one, too."

"You don't have to."

"I want to," said Jarrett. "Good things should be shared." He took the flowers into the kitchen, filled a jar with water and set them on the table. Maybe the boy had spotted him when he'd boosted the roses out of the hearse? Were these roses a gift, he wondered? But, boys didn't give each other flowers. Maybe they were a warning? Jarrett didn't know what to feel, but now he had Martin to think of.

Martin stood at the little fire, warming her hands in its flickering glow like Robby had crouched at his candle.

"Um?" asked Jarrett. "Can I take your hoodie? ...I mean hang it up."

"Thank you." Martin slipped the tote off her shoulder and took off the rain-soaked hoodie. She was wearing her old black tee underneath, and her honey-bronze tummy was peeking a bit. Jarrett hung the hoodie above the fire, where it dripped hissing drops in the flames, and Martin unzipped the tote.

"Dad found this for you," she said, pulling out a Mac laptop. "It had some maggots in it, but I cleaned it up an' charged it. The battery's good, an' it works okay. Must have been a little kid's, there's an Elmo program. But I added some apps you can use for homework."

"Thanks!" said Jarrett. "It look almost new."

"It's about four years old," said Martin. "The kid probably got a new one."

118

"I put it on the kitchen table an' make us that coffee," said Jarrett.

Martin spread her palms to the flames again. "I'll stay here a minute an' warm up a little."

"I was just gonna start on my homework," said Jarrett, padding into the kitchen. "Got at least a hour to do. ...Guess you fly in Science?"

"It's important for bein' a doctor," said Martin. "Our school ain't really teachin' much, an' the book is pretty outdated, but you never know what you gonna learn."

"That's kinda profound," said Jarrett. He set the computer on the table next to the roses in the jar. "Can you show me how to work it? It ain't like the desktops at school."

"Which *should* be at the dump," said Martin. "But it works about the same except for the finger mouse."

Jarrett opened the Mac and found the power switch. Elmo appeared at startup, sounding slightly insane. "Computer fun is sometimes fun. Did you go out and play today?"

"No, I worked my ass off," said Jarrett, and Martin giggled.

Jarrett got mugs from a cupboard, spooned in instant coffee and filled them from the kettle. Martin asked, "Is that a funeral home next door?"

"Yeah," said Jarrett. "It was closed before I was born, but look like it gonna open again."

"Plenty of business in this neighborhood. But, it looks like a family lives there... nice an' pretty an' all the flowers... except for the hearse in the driveway."

"Yeah," agreed Jarrett. "But it really too nice for this 'hood. That why you know it's a death house."

"Is that your room?" asked Martin, checking the broken door.

"Yeah," said Jarrett

"Mind if I peep?"

"Go ahead, but it kinda messy."

The laptop squeaked, "Elmo always cleans up his room before he has computer fun!"

Martin giggled. "Elmo would shit if he saw mine."

Jarrett tried to get rid of Elmo as Martin scoped around in his room. He wondered if she could feel its chill.

"I guess that's the window?" called Martin. "Where you cut your arm?"

"Yeah."

"Must be a bad memory."

Elmo said, "If you see something scary tell mom or dad!"

"Sorta," said Jarrett. "...Um, cold in there, ain't it?"

"Not really," said Martin. "Except for the draft from the window." There was a pause, then she laughed. "You do this cartoon of yourself?"

"Nah," said Jarrett. "The cool fat dude at the bakery done it. 'Member I told you 'bout him... Double-D?"

"Being overweight is unhealthy," said Elmo.

"Looks just like you," said Martin. "Now I know what you mean about havin' a tail. ...You build this model airplane?"

"Yeah, but a long time ago."

Martin returned to the living room and picked something up off the floor. "This key important?" she asked, coming into the kitchen.

"Musta fell out my pocket. Thanks." Jarrett put the key beside the roses. "Oh, sorry. Sit down."

"Thanks." Martin glanced at the clock. "I didn't know it was gettin' this late. Maybe I shouldn't have bothered you."

Elmo said, "Kids need lots of sleep to stay healthy."

"You're not," said Jarrett. "I don't gotta get up 'till seven. You?"

Martin sipped coffee. "Same." She picked up Jarrett's Science book. "There's only ten questions at the end of the chapter. I could read 'em to you if you want. You could put the answers on the computer. Piece of cake."

"If I can ever lose Elmo," said Jarrett, still fiddling with the keyboard.

"Pull him into the trash."

"I tried but he keeps poppin' out. ...Speakin' of cake, you like some?"

Martin smiled and patted her tummy. "Cake is an anytime food for me."

120

TWENTY-ONE

Jarrett got plates, forks and a knife, dished up two hefty wedges of cake, then sat down across from Martin. "There's this homey of mine I think you'd like. He sorta hangs at that peaceful place I been tellin' you about."

Martin nibbled a forkful of frosting. "You sure got me curious about that. I never knew of any park as nice as what you been sayin'."

"Um... we could go there tomorrow. After school, if it ain't rainin'."

"What about your job?"

"I made the rent today. An' a little more. ...What about your job at the Center?"

"Even God took a day off to rest."

Jarrett picked up his fork, then glanced down at himself. "I'ma go put on a shirt."

"You don't have to," said Martin. "I've seen this much of you already."

"But, we here in my crib."

"Are you different here? I don't see a tail."

Elmo squeaked, "Pretending is fun but it's not real!"

"*You* sure as hell ain't." Jarrett turned off the computer. Then he thought of the chill in his room and the eerie feeling of being watched. But he didn't want to talk about that.

"What if the man came back?" asked Martin.

The question was so unexpected that Jarrett almost dropped his fork. But then he frowned. "What kinda question is that?"

"Hypothetical, I guess."

Jarrett considered. "I don't know what I'd do. I could say I'd throw his ass out. ...Like I *should* of done the first day he come here."

"But you couldn't have," said Martin. "An' don't puff your chest an' deny it. That's why you were scared tonight, huh?"

"How you know I was scared?"

"You sounded scared when you answered the bell."

"I thought it was the cop."

Martin studied Jarrett's face. "That's scary enough. But I think there's somethin' else scaring you. I think you're feelin' guilty for not doing somethin' you couldn't have done. An' now it's come back to haunt you."

"...Well... I coulda got me some steel."

Martin frowned. "That would have been dumb, an' you know it. You'd probably be in prison now. An' Panther-boy would die in a cage."

Jarrett returned Martin's frown. "I would of done somethin' different then if I knew what I know now."

Martin smiled. "Just about everybody would. But, we can only learn from the past, we can't go back an' change it."

Jarrett glanced to his room. "For sure I do somethin' different today. Even if he come back from the grave."

Martin shivered. "I didn't mean *that* hypothetical! Sorry, it was a stupid question."

Jarrett sighed. "No it wasn't. ...Maybe I am blamin' myself for not doin' somethin' I couldn't of done." He glanced to his room again.

Martin followed his eyes. "You look like you're expecting a ghost."

"You believe in ghosts?"

"I will when I see one. Do you?"

"Maybe," said Jarrett. "'Least in ghosts that haunt your mind."

Martin posed like a fortune-teller, peering into her coffee mug. "I sense a presence in this room."

Now it was Jarrett who shivered. "Don't do that. Please." He made himself laugh. "Besides, the ghost ain't hauntin' *this* room."

"Sorry," said Martin. "I keep forgettin' you been through a lot." She looked around. "It might not be good for you, livin' alone."

"Sound like somethin' Elmo would say."

Martin sighed. "Must be nice in his world."

"I'd call it kinda retarded," said Jarrett. "Like believin' in a fairytale where nothin' bad ever happen to kids."

"Privileged anyhow, which is the same thing sometimes, especially if you don't know it." Martin looked around. "There's a lot of bad memories here. I can almost feel 'em myself."

"Like in my room?"

"It's cold because the window's broken. Your mind can play tricks when you're tired. An' you gotta be tired from all that's happened on top of workin' so hard." Martin touched Jarrett's hand across the table. "You could stay at the Center. I do sometimes when I'm workin' late."

"Thanks, but... I think I gotta stay here. Maybe *because* it scare me. ...Like, sometimes you gotta be scared, or how you can you learn to deal with scary? Just like sometimes you gotta be hurt to learn how to deal with hurtin'." Jarrett looked around. "There's a lot of good memories here, too. Me an' my mom were happy. An' my dad." He shrugged. "If there is a ghost in this place... or even just in my mind... I gotta bury it myself. ...Did that make any sense?"

"Lots," said Martin.

"That's cool. 'Cause makin' sense ain't been my thing."

Martin forked more cake. "Makin' sense can be dangerous when everyone else is as clueless as Elmo."

Jarrett laughed. "Yeah, the cop told me not to get smart."

"I think he meant somethin' else."

"But, it come out the same if you think about it."

"Is he still watchin' you?" asked Martin.

"Ain't seen him around the last few days, but I got a feelin' he is. ...Or somebody is, anyway."

"But you didn't do anything wrong."

"*Everything* I do is wrong. If he can't get me for murder, he can still bust me on Elmo's laws. ...Um, he might of seen you come here tonight."

123

Martin shrugged. "Guess I'm an Elmo outlaw, too."

"You think the whole world is like that for us? Laws that make us somethin' we ain't? Like, bad when we only tryin' to live an' doin' the best with what we got?"

Martin took a sip of coffee. "Only one way to find out... get the hell out of here an' go look."

Jarrett dropped his chin to his hands. "Sometimes I think that's the hardest part... gettin' the hell out of here."

"'The longest journey begins with a single step.'"

"That more Shakespeare?"

"Somebody else," said Martin. "I forget who, but I'm sure they're dead. But we could always do a search."

"Mean this computer can go on the web?"

"We can use my account. Where's your phone line?"

"Don't got one no more, 'cause... well, you know."

Martin smiled. "Then we'll do the best with what we got." She picked up Jarrett's Science book and turned the computer on. "An', this is about the only step we can take tonight."

Elmo squeaked, "Computer fun is sometimes fun. Did you go out and play today?"

"Guess it is," said Jarrett. "'Cept for when I walk you home."

"You don't have to, I know you're tired."

"But I want to," said Jarrett. "...Or... you could stay here for the rest of the night." He was surprised he'd said that -- and Elmo looked profoundly shocked -- but went on anyway, "Don't make sense for you to go out an' get wet again. ...'Course, I don't guess your folks would see it that way."

"My mom works the graveyard at Dennys, remember?"

"Oh, yeah. I forgot. ...But, what about your dad?"

"He works double shifts. I'm not the only one in my family who wants to get the hell out of here."

"Surprised you don't got a second job."

"I do," said Martin. "Same as you. It's called school." She seemed to consider. "I'd say we were pretty mature, wouldn't you?"

Jarrett glanced at Elmo, who looked like he'd seen something scary. "Don't seem like we got a choice."

Martin smiled. "The couch looks pretty comfortable. ...Or, were you thinkin' of other arrangements?"

Jarrett smiled, too. "I didn't get that far. Makin' plans ain't been my thing, neither."

"Think you would have? ...Got that far?"

"I don't know. But, I gotta get this homework done if I'm gonna get out of eighth-grade. How mature is that?"

Martin opened the book. "Pretty damn."

TWENTY-TWO

Martin laughed in the afternoon sunlight. "This is about as peaceful a place as kids like us are gonna get."

Jarrett felt good hearing Martin laugh. She had a happy and free kind of laugh that didn't care if Elmo's world heard it. Her laugh was like she dressed and talked; and she'd laughed when she'd woken up on the couch in Jarrett's living room that morning.

Jarrett had slept on the floor by the heater like Panther-boy at his jungle campfire; and Martin seemed to understand why he didn't want to sleep in his room. Breakfast had been coffee and donuts -- Elmo wouldn't have approved -- then they had walked to school together as if they'd been doing it all their lives.

But, after school he'd been worried that Martin might get scared when she found where he was taking her.

She and Jarrett had watched for the cop as they'd walked through the busy late-afternoon streets -- the junkyard noisily shredding car corpses, the blond and black brothers waving to Jarrett, while Satan actually wagged his tail and came to the fence to lick Jarrett's hand. Martin had asked where they were going, but Jarrett said it was a surprise. They had passed the bakery, where the young truck driver tooted his horn while rolling out through the gate, and Jarrett had waved to Double-D who was driving a forklift loaded with cakes and steering one-handed while eating one.

"So, you think it's cool?" asked Jarrett now as they stood at the graveyard gates.

Martin stepped up and took hold of the bars, scanning the grassy, sunlit place with its tottering tombstones and time-weathered angels.

126

"There's a lot more green an' growin' things than I've seen in most parks. ...Is that a pond? Listen to the water. An' birds even singin' in there." Then she studied the massive old lock. "But, how do we get in?"

"Panther-boy's got ways." Jarrett set down the bag he'd brought -- sandwiches, Cokes, and a cream-filled cake -- and pulled the key from his pocket.

Martin raised an eyebrow. "You have a key to a graveyard?"

"It a skeleton key," said Jarrett. "They can open a lot of things." He unlocked the chain to let Martin enter, then followed and closed the gates behind them. "Gotta lock 'em again, people dyin' to get in."

"An' I always thought you were sorta grave." Martin looked around. "Funny, I feel kinda safe in here, an' this isn't the kind of place you'd expect to make you feel that way."

"Maybe 'cause the real scary shit be out there on the street."

Martin asked, "So, this is where your homey hangs out? You've kinda kept him a secret, too."

"I didn't know if you could handle it. The graveyard, I mean," said Jarrett. "But, I guess if you gonna be a doctor, you gonna be seein' lots of dead folks. ...Um, cuttin' 'em open for practice, I mean. Not makin' 'em that way."

"Mrs. Davis took me down to the morgue in the hospital where she works. It was very educational." Martin read the name on a stone. "But not *this* dead, I hope. Died in 1933. Not much left to practice on."

Jarrett turned toward the little stone house with its leafy shroud of blackberry vines. "I hope Robby's here." He shaded his eyes against the sun, searching among the pale angels for a glimpse of warm honey-bronze. "Sometimes he plays in the pond. ...Um, out no clothes on."

Martin smiled. "I'm gonna be lookin' at people's bodies... livin' ones... for most of my life. But, if Robby's as drop-dead fly as you, I think I'd be tempted to join him."

Jarrett glanced down at himself; his ragged old jeans dirty from work, and his sneaks about as battered as Robby's except for not having tape on their toes. His tattered T-shirt had once been white but now looked urban camouflage. "You might think Robby's better-lookin'. He's a lot more huggable than me."

Martin laughed. She wore the same clothes she'd worn last night, the faded jeans and old black Tee. "You're huggable too, but you don't seem to know it."

"Maybe I never practiced enough." Jarrett climbed on an angel's shoulders, cupped his hands to his mouth and called Robby's name.

"Careful," laughed Martin. "You'll wake the dead."

"That ain't been a problem so far." Jarrett called louder. The birds stopped singing as if to listen, but there was only the music of water trickling from the bronze boy's vase. Jarrett hopped down. "Guess he gone out to dig up some grub."

"I'd hate to think he'd dig it up here."

"There's lots of ribs."

Martin made a face. "You been hangin' with an undertaker?"

Jarrett thought of the dark slender boy. For a moment he felt a twinge of fear, recalling the roses left on his steps. "Never even met one. ...Wanna see where Robby live?"

"Wait a minute," said Martin. "You tellin' me Robby *lives* here?"

"Um, yeah. He be homeless. I didn't wanna tell you before."

Martin rolled her eyes. "In case I couldn't handle it?"

"Yeah."

"You'd be surprised at what I can handle. ...Don't you dare make a joke about that!" Martin scanned the graveyard again. "If I didn't know you better, I might think you had an imaginary friend."

"He's real," said Jarrett. "Sometimes it's me I wonder about."

Martin touched Jarrett's arm. "You feel real to me. Unless I'm only imagining you. ...So, where's Robby live?"

Jarrett pointed. "Back there. C'mon."

It seemed natural to take Martin's hand as they walked up the weed-tangled path to the crypt.

"Looks like he's got the best house in the 'hood," said Martin as they climbed the step. She ducked beneath the blackberry vines to study the rusty iron door. "Guess he don't need to lock up, but the crime rate's probably low in here."

"It chained, see?" said Jarrett. "They used to do that in the ol' days. Leave the door open a little so if someone got buried alive they could scream."

"Hopefully somebody heard 'em," said Martin. "I'd hate to wake up in the dark alone an' realize I was in a grave!"

"That would be some kinda hell," agreed Jarrett. He peeped through the narrow gap. Sunlight streamed in through the colored glass window and painted the floor with a rainbow. "Thought he might be takin' a nap but I guess he gone out somewhere. You can see his stuff back in the corner. I spent three nights in there with him."

Martin cocked her head. "How come you can sleep in a grave but not in a 'haunted' room?"

"Guess it depend what's doin' the hauntin'. Besides, in here I wasn't alone."

Martin peered in past Jarrett's shoulder. "Looks like you guys were right at home. I see malt bottles, an' cake wrappers."

"Wanna go in?" asked Jarrett. "Robby won't mind." He laughed. "Neither will nobody else."

Martin pulled on the door, and the heavy chain clanked. "It's not a question of wanting." She patted her tummy. "There's too much of me, an' not enough chain." Her eyes ran over Jarrett's chest. "Must be a tight squeeze even for you. Robby can't be all that chubby. Not like you described him."

"He's soft an' rolly," said Jarrett. "'Squeezably soft,' like they say on TV."

"Small bones," said Martin. "But if you keep bringin' him cakes he's gonna eat himself out of a home."

Jarrett pushed the door shut. "I been axin' him to come home with me, but I think he's scared to leave this place."

"Why would he be scared to leave? Most people would be scared to stay."

"Robby got caught in some gang-bangin' shit. Had to kill another kid or he woulda got capped himself. Why I been keepin' this place on the under. Don't want that detective snoopin' around diggin' up trouble for Robby."

"Oh," said Martin. Her face saddened. "Almost like his life was

129

over before it really began."

"Yeah, an' that sucks," said Jarrett.

"How long ago did it happen?"

"He never said, but I didn't axe."

Martin looked out at the sunny graveyard through the green curtain of blackberry vines. "This doesn't seem like a bad place, for what it is anyhow, but he can't have much of a life in here."

"I told him that, too," said Jarrett. Then he had a new thought. "Maybe it's been so long since it happen the cops forgot about it? Like, he's only hidin' from a ghost."

"This would be the last place on earth where I'd try to hide from a ghost." Martin considered. "But, a year can make a lot of difference in how somebody looks at our age. Maybe the cops wouldn't recognize him."

"An' he like to eat," said Jarrett. "We could help him get fatter this summer so nobody'd recognize him."

Martin nodded. "He could probably start a whole new life if there was somebody to help."

"He said one his homies had a plan for gettin' him outta here, but I don't think it's gonna happen."

"We could tell Mrs. Davis," said Martin. "She's helped lots of people come back to life."

"An' maybe he'll listen to you," said Jarrett. "You got a way of makin' sense. He's gotta come back pretty soon. Wanna go sit by the pond an' wait?"

"Sure," said Martin.

They walked down the path to the pond and sat on Christopher Angel's grave. Bees hummed over the flowers, and the trickling splash from the water boy's vase made a soothing musical sound. The air smelled fresh from last night's rain, and the sun was warm and bright. They ate the sandwiches Martin had made, then messily shared the cake.

Martin regarded her frosted hand; and Jarrett said, "Sorry, I should of brought napkins."

"I can lick my fingers," said Martin. "That always gives mom the fits."

"Won't bother me," said Jarrett, who'd already licked his own. "I lick 'em for you if you want?"

Martin smiled. "I'm scared you'd bite. You got a hungry kinda look."

Jarrett frowned for a moment. "I had lots of practice lookin' hungry." Then he smiled again. "You didn't think I was dangerous when you was alone in my crib last night."

"I wasn't alone, you were there. But, you're different in here."

"What you mean?"

Martin studied Jarrett. "I'm not sure. ...If this wasn't a graveyard, I'd say you belonged here."

"Funny," said Jarrett. "I feel that way too when I'm here with Robby." He turned toward the little stone house. "I almost died in there." He tried to recall the rainy night, dragging himself to the graveyard gates, beaten, bloody, shivering, like a baby left on the doorstep of Death. "Maybe I did an' I just don't know it? ...That was a wack thing to say."

"It makes sense," said Martin. "Like a near-death experience. Different things happen to different people. Some see ghosts, some see heaven... or at least what they think is heaven. But it usually changes their lives somehow."

Jarrett was silent a moment or two. "Maybe you right," he said at last. "When I was outside them gates that night, Robby said he could almost see through me. Maybe that means I was halfway dead? Like, havin' one foot in the grave?"

Martin smiled. "You must have pulled it out again, or else you'd still be in there. An' after this long you wouldn't be pretty!"

Jarrett gazed at the vine-covered crypt. "Maybe part of me *is* still in there? Like, part of my spirit... or maybe my soul."

TWENTY-THREE

"I like what's out here now," said Martin. She washed her hands in the pond then studied the sparkling water. "It would be cool to go wading."

"Want to?" asked Jarrett.

"What about broken bottles an' trash?"

"I don't think there's none of that here. Not like in the city park. Me an' Robby run around barefoot an' wrestled in that pond."

Martin seemed to be picturing that. "More than barefoot?"

"Well... yeah. But, it wasn't mixed company."

Martin laughed. "Except for girl ghosts." In moments she and Jarrett were barefoot, their jeans rolled up past their knees and wading hand-and-hand in the water. Martin studied the chubby bronze boy. "He's anatomically-correct."

"I noticed that," said Jarrett.

"You could take off your shirt," suggested Martin.

"Yeah, but it don't seem fair."

"Why not?"

"Well, the sun just as warm for you, ain't it?"

"Sure, but girls don't get to go shirtless."

"Wonder whose idea that was?"

"Somebody like Elmo, I'm sure," said Martin. "But, I like lookin' at you. An' that's a better gift than a rose 'cause you ain't gonna wilt away."

Jarrett pulled off his shirt., and like that first day at the center, he felt Martin's eyes like a warm sensation. "I like lookin' at you," he said, then faced the smiling water boy. "But it still ain't fair. You seen

132

most of me an' all of him, but I got to imagine a lot of you."

Martin giggled. "There's a lot of me to imagine."

Jarrett laughed. "An' all of it good, outside an' inside."

They went back to sit on Christopher's grave, and Martin turned toward the gates. "A lot of things out there aren't fair. But, somehow it's different in here. It's like, if somebody came up to those gates, they couldn't see either one of us now. ...Maybe there's some kinda magic in here?"

"You believe in magic?" asked Jarrett. "I thought you believed in God."

"God is magic," said Martin. "Like, when I see the sun comin' up, or the stars at night. Or all these pretty flowers in here. ...Or meet someone like you. That's God's magic to me." She looked up at Christopher's sad stone face. "I don't need angels playin' harps."

Martin gazed around again. "Maybe there's other places like this... green an' peaceful an' safe. Maybe for people to rest in a while, to get back their strength to go on with their lives."

"Like God's rehab centers," said Jarrett. "An' maybe this one is a graveyard 'cause it's the only peaceful place kids like us can find."

He drew a deep breath of the life-scented air. The sun played over his midnight skin, and he suddenly wanted to leap over headstones and dance upon tombs... maybe like a way to thank God for giving him a life. He felt Martin's eyes again. "That feels good. Bein' looked at instead of looked through."

"Feels good when you do it back," said Martin.

"Feels good doin' it back," said Jarrett. "Even what I gotta imagine. ...Um, would a hug be okay in here?"

Martin opened her arms. "A hug would be okay anywhere."

The afternoon passed away in peace to the soothing sounds of trickling water and gentle humming of bees. But, Jarrett and Martin were going somewhere, each new sensation a magical door that opened and led to another until...

Jarrett drew away, his breathing a little fast. "Guess that as far as we better go."

Martin, also breathing fast, lay back against the tombstone. "Maybe it is."

Jarrett sighed. "Didn't know there was a maybe."

"We've got a choice. That makes it a maybe."

"...Oh," said Jarrett. "But, last night we was bein' mature." He lay down in the grass on his belly, feeling almost too full of life, his dread-locks making a secret place from which he gazed at Martin. "We ain't Elmo's clueless kids; we know what can happen."

"I thought about that," said Martin. "I've been thinking about it since last night. ...Or really since I met you."

"I have, too," said Jarrett. "Even when I didn't know it."

Martin gazed up at the evening sky, but Jarrett remained where he was. If he'd really had a tail it would have been whipping back and forth. The shadow cast by Christopher Angel showed it was getting near six o'clock, though the sun was still warm on Jarrett's back. When would Robby return, he wondered? He wanted Martin to meet him... and now more than ever because there was hope. Martin's voice surprised him:

"It's still a maybe."

"Huh?" said Jarrett.

"Like you said, we're not Elmo's kids."

"...Oh," said Jarrett. "Um... fact is, I got one. I snuck out at lunch to a store. I got real good at sneakin' this year."

"How come you never said?" asked Martin.

"Didn't seem right to go whippin' it out."

"'Cause you figured I couldn't handle it?"

"I thought you might think it was all I wanted. Like, bringin' you here to jump your bones."

Martin looked toward the gates. "Maybe we're all dead out there. Same as these people in here in a way."

"What you mean?" asked Jarrett.

Martin regarded the statues and stones, the crumbling crypts and sad-looking angels. "Everyone buried so close to each other, but nobody touches an' nobody talks."

Jarrett nodded. "Robby told me somethin' like that: 'The grave is a fine an' private place, but none I think do there embrace.'"

"Well," said Martin. "A lot of people out there never touch, or talk in a real live way. An' it's way too late for the people in here, but you an' me are alive in all the ways that matter."

"Sure you want to, Martin? I know it's different with girls... the first time, what I sayin'."

"Thank you."

"Huh?"

"For the compliment. It's somethin' worthy of Panther-boy."

"...Oh... But, what I mean is, they say you always remember the first time. Like, all your life. An'... Well... Seem like to me... for a girl, what I sayin'... it be like givin' a gift. An' one you can only give once."

Martin smiled. "That's why I'd give it to you, But you'd be givin' me a gift, too."

"Um... dudes don't think that way," said Jarrett. "'Least no dude I know." He turned to the chubby water boy as if he might give him a clue, but the boy just smiled in the golden sun.

"Funny," said Jarrett. "We could of just gone to where we was goin'. Like, 'out axin' no questions."

"We already know some of the answers an' most of the maybes," said Martin.

Jarrett took Martin's hand and pointed to the gates. "We got us lots of time out there."

"What do you want to be out there?"

Jarrett considered. "I don't know. An' I didn't think much about it this year. For a while, when I was little, I wanted to be an airplane pilot. Not jet planes, but the kind with propellers. They still flyin' those in places like Africa. Like the model I built."

Martin cocked her head. "We've been talkin' all week about all kinds of stuff. How come you never told me that?"

Jarrett shrugged. "It was just a dream. An' after I got older I figured I wasn't good enough to ever make it happen."

Martin frowned. "Who in hell said you weren't good enough?"

"TV, teachers, cops, an' movies. You don't see black men flyin' airplanes, except Will Smith an' that wasn't real. Even my friends thought I was wack."

Martin thought for a moment. "There must be lots of black pilots, but you hardly ever see any... like you said on TV an' movies. Or read about 'em in books. Not for role-models of what we can be."

135

Jarrett nodded. "You don't see cartoons like Double-D's of black kids bein' heroes neither." He looked around the graveyard. "Or read about kids like you an' me doin' stuff like this."

"I've never seen brothers build boats," said Martin. "But you told me about them."

"Ever seen a brother plant flowers?"

"Not a young one."

"Probably scared to," said Jarrett. "'Cause they think that wouldn't be 'black' by what's out there says black should be."

"Would Panther-boy plant a flower... out there?"

"Maybe I will before mom comes home.... build a box in the livin' room window so she could see 'em every day."

"How about goin' to college?" asked Martin. "Does that scare Panther-boy?"

"Take money, what don't?"

"But, you're Panther-boy."

Jarrett smiled. "Sometimes I forget."

Martin reached down in the grass. "Panther-boy's key fell out of his pocket.".

"Still got my real one, just like you." Jarrett tapped his forehead with a fingertip. "Right here in my skull."

"Better hold onto this one, too. It unlocks the gates to this place, an' we can come back when we need to rest from all the shit out there." Martin unwound a strip from her bracelet, tied the big key like a necklace charm and slipped it over Jarrett's head, where it hung like a clapper between muscle bells. Jarrett moved close and kissed Martin's lips.

They could have gone on from there, he thought. But they had lots of time to make choices... to *think* about choices and make the right ones. He looked to the graveyard gates again: the rosy sun of early evening had turned the rusty bars to gold.

"You thinkin' about Robby?" asked Martin, resting her head on Jarrett's shoulder.

Jarrett watched the shadows deepen among the silent angels. "You got a future on the way. Maybe I can make one. But Robby don't got nothin'."

"He's got you," said Martin. "Let's wait a while longer."

"Gonna be dark pretty soon."

Martin nestled against him and touched the key on his chest. "I'm not afraid of ghosts with Panther-boy beside me."

TWENTY-FOUR

It was raining hard on Saturday evening as Jarrett left work around seven o'clock. The darkening streets were shrouded in fog that chilled his bones as he skated home. Yet, cold and wet in his sodden clothes, his breath puffing steam as he ran up the stairs, he felt Panther-boy proud to be paying the rent with money he'd earned with his muscles and mind.

The landlord, who looked like a gloomy old ghoul, dug up a smile while counting the cash and hoped Jarrett's "troubles" were over. Jarrett's mom would be home in a week, and Mrs. Davis had found her a job in the hospital cafeteria. The pay was good and there was free food, which covered two of life's basic needs.

He went out again for a bucket of chicken and a box of candles for Robby, who hadn't returned the night before, though Jarrett and Martin had waited for hours, passing the time in each other's arms and not a bit scared to talk about life in that shadowy place of the dead.

It was still raining hard as Jarrett skated back to his house, swooshing through puddles and jumping gutters. He'd planned to head straight for the graveyard, but his soaking clothes were cold as ice and it didn't make sense to catch his death... not with a future to live for. He scanned around for the rat-colored car as he rolled down the half-flooded sidewalk. He hadn't seen the detective again, not since facing him out on the street, and he wondered if his case was closed, though he doubted if Locke would bother to tell him.

He'd left the gas fire burning, and the living room was comfortably warm as he stripped in front of the whispering flames.

138

He stayed there a while, his palms held out, hearing the rush and patter of rain and its trickling splash as it poured off the roof to rattle the garbage cans in the alley. His dreadlocks dripped on his shoulders and chest, and glistening rivulets ran down his body to spatter the floor at his feet. He wondered if Robby was warm and dry.

He was determined to bring Robby home and back to the land of the living. It was Panther-boy's next mission. He'd already asked his mother about taking in his homeless friend; and Martin was sure Mrs. Davis would help, but he had to make Robby believe in him instead of waiting for Eric.

The fire's warmth felt good on his skin, and the sound of the rain was soothing. Feeling at peace, he thought of Martin and what they had done yesterday. Also what they hadn't done.

Was that a door he should have opened, a lock he and Martin should have unlocked? Jarrett fingered the skeleton key that swung between his stony pecs. He remembered how Martin had looked in the sunlight, her warm-glowing, honey-bronze, huggable shape. He looked at the couch where she'd slept Thursday night, and remembered the roses she'd found on the porch. The funeral home boy *must* have left them... but why?

He padded into his room, which seemed almost normally warm tonight in spite of the rain and salt-scented breeze. Had the ghost passed on, he wondered? ...Or was it just watching to see if he weakened before coming back to haunt him again?

He glanced at the Panther-boy cartoon, then went to the broken window. Droplets glittered like molten gold on what remained of the glass. He gazed through the shimmering curtain of rain to the flower-filled yard of the funeral home, surprised to see its front windows alight, their heavy drapes glowing a deep purple shade. He noted the hearse's back door was open, and there were more flowers inside. Then, the dark boy appeared on the porch in a dim fan of light from the doorway. He was clad in his long leather coat again... and bearing the coffin on one slender shoulder.

He didn't seem to notice the rain as he carried the coffin across the lawn and slid it gently into the hearse. Jarrett wondered if it was empty: despite his finely-sculpted muscles, the boy just didn't look strong enough to carry a coffin containing... remains.

After closing the hearse's door, the boy glanced up at Jarrett's window, as if he'd felt Jarrett watching him. His face was only a shadow beneath his halo of thistledown hair that sparkled with rainwater jewels. Jarrett felt uneasy, as if the boy knew something about him he didn't know himself. He remembered the scene in the viewing room, the candles, the coffin, the slim boy asleep... and maybe questions he should have asked. He almost stepped back from the window, but the boy got into the hearse, started the engine and rolled away. Jarrett watched the long black car pushing a wave down the flooded street until its ruby tail lights vanished, fading into the rain.

It was getting close to midnight. He'd put on dry clothes and snagged Robby's board when the door buzzer sounded a jarring note. Jarrett froze for a second, feeling an icy tingle of fear, but then he flipped the speaker switch. "Martin?"

"Jarrett Ross."

It could have been the voice of Death! The air in the room went as cold as a grave, and a skeleton finger ran down Jarrett's spine. It took a second to make his voice work.

"What you want?" he asked.

"Just open the door," said Locke.

But Jarrett raced for his room! Using Robby's board, he smashed the remains of the window glass and scrambled out to the rain-slicked roof. The worn-out soles of his sneakers slipped and he almost fell off the edge, but managed to grab the window frame. Then he scuttled along to the back of the house and dropped from the eaves to a Dumpster. The cop must have heard the breaking glass, or the hollow boom of the Dumpster lid. Footsteps sounded, splashing through puddles. A shadow appeared at the alley mouth.

"Jarrett! Stop!"

But, Jarrett dashed away down the alley, dodging more Dumpsters and cans in the dark. The ghost in his room had been waiting for this! There was only one safe place in the world!

He heard a car start up behind him and roar away to circle the

140

block as he reached the street at the end of the alley. He decked Robby's board and shot into the mist. The fog flashed pearly gray at his back as the car came squealing around the corner, red light flashing, siren wailing, but Jarrett cut into another alley, frantically kicking with all his strength. He skidded on trash and crashed to the ground, slamming into a garbage can as the car slewed into the alley mouth, its headlights stabbing the fog. He scrambled up and recovered the board, decking and kicking away again, reaching yet another street as the cop car slid to a shrieking halt, a Dumpster blocking its path.

"Jarrett...!" The detective's voice was lost in the fog as Jarrett rolled on through the night. He cut through more alleys and chose darker streets. He heard the detective's car several times, its siren seeming to scream in rage but lagging farther and farther behind until he finally heard it no more. The rain had slackened to less than a drizzle, but fog was still drifting in from the bay, and the feeble street lamps wore halos of gold.

The heavy mist smothered the sound of his wheels as Jarrett neared the graveyard gates with steam curling up from his sweating body. The street lamp was only a dim yellow blur, and the wet wires sputtered and buzzed overhead. The gutter drains were choked with trash, and the end of the street was a murky lake, what little of it could be seen. Jarrett waded the rest of the way through oily water up to his ankles. He paused to listen for sounds of pursuit, but he seemed to have lost the hunter... and this time maybe forever.

He gripped the cold bars and peered into the graveyard. Mist drifted thick though the weed-tangled grounds, shrouding the tombstones and cloaking the statues beyond the faint glow of the one lonely lamp. He slipped the skeleton key from his neck, unlocked the lock and pushed the gates open, wincing at their rusty scream but feeling a little safer after locking them behind him.

The fog was growing thicker as he started for Robby's crypt, pushing his way through dripping weeds and trying to stay on the tangled path. He took a wrong turn in the darkness and found himself facing Christopher Angel beside the dimly glimmering pond. The boy was weeping raindrop tears that fell on the little grave. Jarrett drew back from the sad stone face and lost his sense of direction. He couldn't see the light anymore as the fog closed in around him. He tripped on a crumbling marble slab and fell on another grave. For a moment he was afraid. But that was stupid, he told himself. He'd been here only yesterday in the evening sun with Martin. And he'd hugged Robby here in the grass.

And now this place would be his home, too. Like Robby, he was dead to a world that didn't want him to live.

TWENTY-FIVE

Jarrett got to his feet and moved cautiously on, breathing a smoky sigh of relief when he found himself back at the edge of the pond. The fog was too thick to see the bronze boy, but the trickle of water was comforting. Jarrett slowly circled the pond and finally found the path again. At last he pushed through the blackberry vines and onto the crypt's little porch.

The door was shut and the window was dark, but Robby was probably sleeping. Jarrett rapped on the rusty iron, though his knuckles hardly made a sound. "Robby?" he called.

No answer.

Was Robby out hunting for food, Jarrett wondered? And should he go in uninvited? He pictured Robby in his mind -- the cheerful smile, the careless giggle, the huggable, chubby lion-cub look -- and decided it would be cool. Besides, he needed Robby's help, and that was sadly funny because, less than an hour ago, he'd been on his way to help Robby.

The hinges made a ghastly screech as he pulled the door open as far as he could against its massive chain. That almost wasn't far enough; his chest had grown from a week of hard work. He shed his coat and stripped off his shirt to wiggle through in jeans and skin. He still might not have made it if he hadn't been slick with rain.

He took out the box of waterproof matches, but paused before striking one. He held his breath and listened, but heard no sign of life. Still, he called softly, "Robby?"

Only the silence of stone.

He struck a match. The tomb was empty except for Robby's blan-

143

kets and books. Jarrett crouched to light the candle. Its flickering glow seemed as friendly as ever, chasing shadows to cobwebby corners. It cheerfully winked from the flower vases and heavy brass pulls on the drawer-like slabs. But, Jarrett's eyes went to the nameless slab. He shivered to think what lay inside. ...But those bones had once been a friend of Robby's, and any friend of Robby's probably wouldn't be scary.

Whether or not they had skin.

Jarrett returned to the doorway and pulled his things through the gap. His shirt was soaked with rain and sweat so he only put his coat back on. Then he sat down to wait for Robby. He studied the nameless slab again. His voice sounded small surrounded by stone, as if he was calling from far away and only hearing an echo: "Um, sorry I don't know your name in there."

His voice seemed to trouble the silence. He glanced at the dusty magic books and remembered what he'd said to Robby about speaking a spell by accident and maybe awakening something. He looked through the age-yellowed comics, but all were too rotted to read. Almost warily, he picked up *The Seventh Book Of Moses*. A place had been marked with a scrap of paper... a spell for calling up the dead!

Jarrett dropped the book and picked up the Bible. Robby had said there were spells in it, too, but Martin had said it was God's magic. The old-fashioned language was hard to follow; something about not going to heaven unless you became as a little child. What did that mean? That every child was innocent until the world made them guilty?

Fingers of fog were invading the crypt, curling in around the door and hovering over the candle flame like spirits seeking warmth. Jarrett got up and dragged the door shut, then sat down again with his hands in his pockets. The only sounds were the dripping of rain and the candle's occasional sputter. Where was Robby tonight?

He opened the Bible again. Some brittle old sheets of binder paper fluttered out on the floor. Jarrett saw pictures of cartoon kids! He snatched them up and his eyes flew wide. The drawings were dim and faded with age, yet he recognized them! They were the gang that wasn't! The boys who Robby had told him about!

144

There was Kevin, lean and mean... *who now drove a bakery truck!*

There were the boys in the scrap yard... *Whitey and Weasel,* who were building a boat!

There was Donny, awesomely fat... *Double-D, who'd drawn these cartoons!*

There was Randy Davis... Randers!... *Mrs. Davis's muscular son!*

And there was another boy, too, midnight-black and willowy slender... *the boy in the funeral home!*

Jarrett stared at the drawings, time-faded, tattered, but true to life. He gazed the slender boy's image the longest... *Eric! The dude who Robby was waiting for!*

...But, how could that be? Robby was only thirteen, about the same age as these cartoon kids... *but all those dudes in real-life were seven years older now!*

Jarrett studied the drawings again, holding them close to the candle flame. Had Robby been lying about living here? Or maybe just playing a game? Like something a lonely kid might do. Jarrett didn't want to believe it, but now it began to make sense. ...Like, how could a homeless kid stay chubby?

Jarrett considered: Double-D might have been giving him food, but why hadn't Robby told Jarrett about it? He'd known Jarrett was hungry, and Double-D gave food to kids. But, if Robby knew Double-D, then why hadn't Double-D said anything when Jarrett had described Robby?

Jarrett tried to figure it out... had Robby only found these cartoons and made those dudes his make-believe friends? The bakery wasn't far away, and Double-D might have lost them. The wind might have blown them into the graveyard. ...Or, Double-D might have thrown them away as his drawing skills improved. These old cartoons were good, but nowhere as good as the Panther-boy sketch or the others Jarrett had seen.

He looked around in the candle glow: the blanket he'd brought was fairly clean but the others were furry with dust. He picked one up and found it rotten. He checked the books and comics again... there was *nothing* in the crypt that wasn't many years old.

Except the things he'd brought.

Why hadn't he noticed that before? ...Because he'd been looking at Robby, watching his cheerful chubby face, seeing only his friendly smile and hearing his careless giggle? ...But, why would Robby lie to him, especially after saving his life?

He got to his feet and went to the window, the window where Robby had first seen him, bloody, half dead, at the graveyard gates.

But, no one could see through that thick colored glass!

Jarrett stood there trying to think as rain pattered softly outside. Had Robby come from some other town, or maybe just a different 'hood? Maybe to stay with a relative because there was trouble at home? He'd said his dad had run away, and then his mom had died. Then he'd escaped from a project home and the gang that wasn't had taken him in.

But, there *wasn't* a gang that wasn't! ...Not anymore: those dudes were all grown and living their lives.

Jarrett fingered the key on his chest as he tried to figure things out. How much of Robby's story was true? Had he really killed a kid and come here to live on the under?

Jarrett glanced back at the dusty old blankets. *Someone* had cribbed in this crypt for a while, sat by the candle, read comics and books, and probably slept in those blankets. He pushed the heavy door open, wincing at the rusty screech, and studied the gap allowed by the chain. That someone had to have been a kid because nobody big could have gotten in.

But, that didn't prove Robby lived here. He might only come to rest in peace. To read his books and sit in the sun in a place where nobody bothered kids... sort of a sometimes heaven.

Jarrett tried to make sense of this thing, leaning with his back to the door while mist curled in around him. Even if Robby had found those cartoons and brought them to life in his mind, the dudes at the junkyard were real. So was Randy Davis. And Double-D and Kevin. And Eric in the funeral home.

And, even if Robby had told a few tales -- maybe his own kind of *Tales From The Crypt* -- he *had* saved Jarrett's life on the real.

Jarrett looked at the nameless slab. Robby could have been

146

telling part of the truth: maybe some kids had really buried another kid in there? A homeless kid who'd been capped on the street and had no one to bury him. And they'd been the gang that wasn't... back when they were Robby's age. Maybe Robby had met Double-D -- who'd been Donny back in the day -- and Double-D had told him the story? And if Robby had killed a kid -- but many years later, of course -- then Double-D might be keeping the secret. So, even if Robby didn't live here, he'd still be staying on the low and this would be a good place to hide.

Jarrett regarded the unmarked slab. There might be a way to check Robby's story. If there was nothing behind that stone, then Robby had just been making things up. Maybe he'd done it to help Jarrett, like stories in books could help people? It *had* helped Jarrett... until the cop had come tonight to take his life away.

He took off his coat and stepped to the slab. He spread his arms to grasp the handles. They felt icy cold. He gave them a cautious pull, but the marble panel didn't budge. It looked like it hadn't been opened in years. Maybe in decades.

Maybe never.

He sucked a deep breath and braced his feet. Then, arching his back, teeth barred in a snarl, he strained at the slab with all his strength. Dust sifted out around the seams, and the panel moved!

An inch.

Sweat broke out on Jarrett's skin despite the midnight cold. He dropped the handles and stood there panting, staring down at a crack of darkness. The skeleton key swung to and fro between the ebony stones of his chest. Slowly, he recovered his breath. Then he bent close to the gap and sniffed... only the dry scent of dust. He picked up the candle and tried to look in, but the flickering glow wasn't bright enough. He wiped sweat from his face and shook back his dreads, scattering drops of molten gold. He set the candle on the floor, sucked another deeper breath, grabbed the handles, braced his feet, and pulled with all his strength. His muscles stood out in stark definition. Steam curled up from his straining body.

With a gritty rasp of stone upon stone, the panel slid suddenly open!

147

But Jarrett shied back from that long dark place. What was he going to see? A grisly thing... or nothing at all? His hand shook as he picked up the candle. He raised the flame high and looked in.

He screamed and leaped back, dropping the candle. The flame went out and he was in darkness!

Spinning around, he lunged for the door, struggling out, raking his chest. He burst through the brambles and leaped from the porch, running blindly into the fog.

He thought he'd been ready to face anything, but he'd never dreamed what lay inside that long dark place of stone!

TWENTY-SIX

Where was the light? The way out here! He ran in darkness, gasping for breath. He slammed into headstones, tripped over tombs and crashed into crumbling angels. He slipped in the grass and fell by the pond, but scrambled up and ran on. Sad stone faces swam out of the mist, weeping glimmering raindrop tears. But at last he saw the street lamp's glow. He was almost past the mossy stone where Robby always sat when a tall dark shape seemed to rise from the grave! He tried to dodge away, but hands reached out and caught him!

"NO!" he yelled, frantically fighting whatever it was.

He heard his own name but was too scared to think.

"Jarrett!" the voice said again.

For a moment the terror he'd felt in the tomb was replaced by the fear of what waited outside. "I didn't do nothin' wrong!" he cried.

"Maybe not," said Detective Locke, relaxing his grip as Jarrett stopped fighting. He slipped the cuffs back in his overcoat pocket. "I could bust you for a lot of things: underage drinking, no guardian, illegal and hazardous employment." He glanced around. "Maybe even grave-robbing. ...But not for murder. That's what I came to tell you tonight when you ran like a scared little rabbit."

Despite his horror of moments before, Jarrett felt anger instead of relief. "I'm tryin' to live, goddammit!"

"Strange kind of place for that, don't you think? ...What are you doing here, anyway?"

"...I... come to see a friend."

149

For a moment Locke looked confused, an expression you seldom saw on a cop, but then he raised an eyebrow. "Must be an *old* friend, kid. There hasn't been a burial here in over fifty years. The city's been wanting to move these graves... or at least what's in 'em... up in the hills."

Jarrett turned toward the little stone house with its leafy shroud of blackberry vines. He fought to keep his voice steady. "You wouldn't understand."

"Don't make that your epitaph, kid. Nobody will *ever* understand if you don't give them a chance." The detective glanced around again. "I don't believe in ghosts, but I wouldn't spend a night in here if you paid me double overtime. ...Which, by the way, I'm not getting."

Jarrett sighed a ghost of steam. "The dead can't hurt you, only the livin'."

"I'll take that under advisement. ...So, what were you running from?"

"...Thought I seen somethin' scary."

"You picked the right location."

"So, am I free?"

"For the present, kid," said Locke. "And if you're as smart as I think you are, maybe you'll stay that way. ...Come on, I'll give you a ride home."

"No. ...Thanks. I walk."

"Life's hard enough, don't make it harder."

"I ain't the one who made it hard."

Locke frowned. "You sure didn't make it easy for me! I figured it was self-defense after the first time I talked to you, but my new boss is 'tough on youth crime.' ...Or you can call a spade a spade, and I think you know what I mean. Wanted to take a bite out of you, and it would have been easy to let him. Instead I busted my butt for a week to prove you weren't just another punk thug. The boss isn't happy you aren't in a cage, but at least my son admitted I might be better than breakfast sausage."

"...Um, thanks," said Jarrett. "You told your son about me?"

"We had a talk about Elmo's law, and he's broken a few. And I

150

aided and abetted since we had a beer."

"Sounds like he's a man," said Jarrett.

"He's working on it. And I'm guilty of trying to keep him a kid." Locke sighed. "Protecting innocent people is supposed to be my job, but I need the truth to do it, and everybody lies to cops, so I had dig up your truth on my own. The only thing I didn't know was where you went at night. You always lost me coming here, so I took a guess tonight. ...That wasn't easy, either. I'm getting too old to be climbing walls."

"I got a key."

"...I won't ask."

They walked to the gates and Jarrett unlocked them. The rat-colored car was almost invisible parked in the half-flooded street in the fog.

"You going be all right, kid?"

Jarrett slipped the key around his neck. "I'm doin' the best with what I got, so I guess that make me a man."

Locke got into his car, but paused before starting the engine. "I didn't make this world, Jarrett, and most of the time I don't like it. I might even like it less than you because I know how it works... and Elmo wouldn't approve. But you better learn how to live out here. The odds are against you, and that's the truth, but it's the only world there is, and the only world worth living in... if you're really a man."

"I take that under advisement."

Jarrett watched as the car drove away, splashing up the flooded street to vanish in the darkness. For a moment he felt a twinge of fear, alone again at the graveyard gates.

"Yo, Jarrett."

For a second Jarrett hoped...

But a tall slender figure came out of the mist. Jarrett was sad but not much surprised. "Whattup, Eric?" he asked.

Eric smiled. Waterdrops sparkled his thistledown hair beneath the haloed street lamp. "Moon, stars, an' us."

"Guess Robby told you my name," said Jarrett.

Eric smiled again. "I know he told you mine."

The fog was thinning a little, and Jarrett saw the long black hearse parked at the end of the street. Then he turned back to gaze at the graveyard. Angels wept with sightless eyes for long-forgotten bones, and the chubby bronze boy went on pouring water. Jarrett shivered, but only with cold.

"Here, man," said Eric. "You don't wanna catch your death when you got so much to live for." He opened his coat and drew Jarrett close.

Jarrett pressed tight to Eric, scenting leather and male sweat, with maybe a ghost of roses. In some other place it might have been strange to be so close to another dude, but here it was only right. "You come for Robby, huh? Like you said you would."

"I come for a dude I used to know an' wish I'd known a lot better, but you're the reason he got to leave."

"Like, get another chance?" asked Jarrett.

"Another key," said Eric, touching the one on Jarrett's chest.

Jarrett sighed. "I just needed him 'cause I was dyin'."

"It's easy to let people die," said Eric. "One way or another. All you gotta do is nothin'. But Robby came to help you live."

"So, there is a way out?" asked Jarrett.

"If there wasn't, it would mean God doesn't care."

Jarrett looked back at the little stone house. Robby wasn't there anymore... only a skeleton, dusty and small. A skeleton clad in ragged jeans, ancient sneakers falling apart with electrical tape on their toes, and an old but newly-washed T-shirt with a smiling, dreadlocked skull on the front.

END

ABOUT THE AUTHOR

Jess Mowry was born in 1960 near Starkville, Mississippi. When he was only a few months old his father took him to live in Oakland, California. Mowry's father was a voracious reader who introduced his son to books at a very early age. Jess attended a public school, but despite his love of reading, dropped out at age thirteen, part way through the eighth grade and worked with his father in the scrap-iron business. In his late teens, Jess moved to Arizona to work as a truck driver and heavy equipment operator. He also lived and worked in Alaska as an engineer aboard a tugboat and as an aircraft mechanic on Douglas C-47 cargo planes, as well as at a children's refuge in Haiti.

Mowry has written twenty-five books and many short stories about black children and teens in a variety of genres, ranging from inner-city settings to the forests of Haiti, the wilds of Alaska, the Arizona desert, the Caribbean Sea, and the African veldt. While some of his novels are set in Oakland and deal with social issues, such as poverty, violence, drugs, gangs, teenage sexuality, and school drop-outs, Mowry has also written ghost tales, as well as novels featuring Voodoo and African magic, in addition to sea stories, and compiled an anthology of Victorian ghost stories.

Jess Mowry lives in Oakland, California.

THIS BOOK IS ALSO AVAILABLE IN A KINDLE EDITION

OTHER ANUBIS BOOKS

AVAILABLE ON AMAZON